'How refreshing—a woman who can still blush.'

'Dr Hunter, if you're not busy, I am. Please leave me to get on with my work.'

'Giving me the brush-off, Clare?' Tom leaned across the desk and took her hands in his. His voice was even deeper and throatier than ever. 'Will you come out to dinner with me tonight? Come out with me tonight; I need to talk, and you're the most relaxing person I've met in years.'

Clare wasn't sure she liked the description. It seemed to indicate he wasn't expecting her to be more than a good listener. It occurred to her that this was perhaps what her own attitude to men indicated. You can't have it both ways, she told herself. A man who respects you *and* high romance.

He seemed to read her thoughts.

'No strings, Clare,' he said softly in his velvet-deep voice. 'Just a pleasant evening, talking shop or whatever you wish.'

'Will you go away and leave me to get on if I say yes?'

'Willingly.'

'Then yes, I'll come out tonight.'

Margaret O'Neill was born in Portsmouth in 1926. She started scribbling at the age of 4 and began nursing at 20. She contracted TB, and when recovered, she did her British Tuberculosis Association nursing training before going on to general training at the Royal Portsmouth Hospital, near the dockyard.

She married another student, a Latvian, and had two children, a son who is now a designer, and a daughter who is an actress and drama teacher. With her late husband she owned and managed several nursing homes, and though now retired, she still has many nursing and medical contacts. Her husband encouraged her writing and would have been delighted to see her books in print. Margaret now lives in Sussex, and loves gardening, reading and writing.

COTTAGE HOSPITAL is her first Medical Romance.

COTTAGE HOSPITAL

BY

MARGARET O'NEILL

MILLS & BOON LIMITED
ETON HOUSE   18–24 PARADISE ROAD
RICHMOND   SURREY   TW9 1SR

First published in Great Britain 1991 by Mills & Boon Limited

© Margaret O'Neill 1991

Australian copyright 1991 Philippine copyright 1991 This edition 1991

ISBN 0 263 77374 4

Set in 10 on 11 pt Linotron Times 03-9108-61551 Typeset in Great Britain by Centracet, Cambridge Made and printed in Great Britain

CHAPTER ONE

CLARE was in the female medical ward when Julie Masters, the new little auxillary nurse, came to tell her that there was a man in her office.

'Cheers,' said Clare cheerfully, much to the nurse's surprise. She was very much in awe of her senior, a sister and, though quite young-looking, acting matron. 'Thank you, Nurse; will you ask him to wait just a minute? I'll be with him shortly. You don't by any chance have a name for this gentleman or a reason why he wants to see me?'

Julie shook her head. 'Sorry, Sister,' she whispered, and, at a nod from Clare, hurried out of the ward.

'Amazing, isn't it?' Staff Nurse Jones said, giving a surperior sniff. 'These untrained people never seem to learn the simplest rule.'

'Oh, come on, Staff, the girl's only just started— give her a chance! I think she has the makings of a good practical nurse. She's a nice, polite little thing, and that counts for much these days.'

'If you say so.'

'Well, I do; now let's get back to Mrs Jackson's leg.' She smiled at the large lady sitting in the chair by her bed. 'I'm going to get Doctor to have a look at this wretched ulcer of yours, Mrs Jackson; see if he can come up with some new treatment. The present medication doesn't seem to be having much effect, does it?'

Mrs Jackson shook her head, and said almost with a kind of pride, 'Nope, nothing seems to touch it, Sister; I've bin 'ere a week now and it's not got no better. It's a real puzzle, isn't it?'

'A medical mystery you are, Mrs Jackson, and no mistake.'

The patient went off into gales of laughter, knowing that Sister Browning was in fact taking the mickey a bit. She was that sort of nurse, always managed to give you a laugh, make you feel better! Mrs Jackson thought that it was a shame that she was stuck in the hospital, looking after sick people all the time, when she ought to be out enjoying herself. She watched the tall slim figure of the sister as she moved away down the ward accompanied by the short, dumpy staff nurse.

''ere,' Mrs Jackson whispered to her neighbour in the next bed. 'She's quite a cracker, isn't she, that there Sister Browning?'

'A very nice young woman and an excellent nurse,' confirmed Miss Carter primly. She might not agree with the way that the patient in the next bed expressed her admiration, but she certainly agreed with her sentiments.

Clare hurried to her office to deal with the visitor. She hoped it wouldn't take long—she was expecting Dr Hunter and his son to appear any minute. The old doctor was to formally hand over the patients into his son's care while he went off for convalescence following a recent heart attack.

She noticed, as she made her way along the long ground-floor corridor of the Cottage Hospital, that it had started to rain. There was a rumble of thunder a long way off, and in the distance, behind the castle, a fork of lightning. She squeezed her eyes shut for a moment. Storms didn't normally bother her, but an incipient headache with all the earmarks of a full-blown migraine made her wince at the thought of flashes of lightning.

The visitor was standing by the window, looking out at the pouring rain and black skies. He turned as she entered. He was wearing an old-fashioned off-white military-looking mackintosh, belted in to a narrow waist. At first she thought that he was very thin, but realised that in fact he was lean and muscular, from his long narrow face to the bottom of his brown brogues. There was no mistaking who he was, though: it just had to be Dr Hunter's son. The same tall leanness, the same blue eyes, slightly faded in the older man, but brilliant in the son. The same shock of thick hair, black with flecks of grey in the man before her, white in the father. She thought that he would be exactly like old Dr Hunter one day, and just prayed that he would be as good a doctor as his father while she had to work with him.

He held out a hand almost before she was in the room. 'Tom Hunter,' he introduced himself. 'And you are, of course, the efficient Miss Browning.'

She nodded. She wasn't sure if she liked the emphasis on efficient—it was as if that were all she was. Not feminine, or pretty, just efficient.

'I thought that Dr Hunter senior was going to bring you over. A sort of formal introduction?'

'What, in this weather, Sister, an elderly man recovering from a heart attack? Not very sensible.'

He made her feel stupid and anything but efficient.

'No, of course not. How is he today?'

'Well, I dare say you know my father, as well as, perhaps better than I. He's making progress, but is a terrible patient—doesn't know what the word convalescence means. I'll be glad to be shot of him up to Scotland and my Aunt Mary. She'll pin him down.' He gave a nice smile which transformed his rather austere expression.

There was another flash of lightning, this time much nearer and much more vivid. Clare automatically closed her eyes.

'Frightened of a little lightning, Sister? You do surprise me after all the build-up my father gave you. Couldn't imagine you being intimidated by anything.'

'I've a headache,' explained Clare coolly, though she felt herself flushing to the roots of her short corn-coloured hair. 'If you'll allow me?' She eased herself past him and sat down at her desk. 'Please, do sit down.'

He removed his wet mac, draping it over one chair as he sat himself down in the other.

'Excuse me.' Clare took two tablets from the drawer and swallowed them with a little water from the glass on her desk. 'To prevent a migraine; I feel one creeping up.' She smiled to let him know that she was capable of dealing with a migraine, and was surprised by his response.

'Oh, you poor girl. You're a migraine subject, and storms certainly don't help. I know from personal experience.'

'Oh, you get migraines too?'

'Not any more,' he said. 'Had my last one about seven years ago. Cured by an old medicine-man in a remote Indian village.'

'My goodness, a cure would be worth a fortune— why didn't you bring it home with you?'

'Because I haven't the faintest idea what it consisted of. Just a filthy brew that did the trick. I'm absolutely sure, though, that half the ingredients simply wouldn't be acceptable to the British pharmacopoeia, and I'd be struck off.'

'Ah, "Eye of newt, and toe of frog" stuff?'

'Something like that.'

They smiled at each other, and Clare thought that they might get along rather well together.

'What would you like to do?' she asked. 'Go through things in general—you know, routines and such—or have a guided tour around the hospital, getting to know the layout and who's working where and so on? I presume that you don't want to plunge into a proper round at this stage.'

'God forbid! Sounds terrifying. It's been years since I did anything like a formal round, you know, white coat and stethoscope stuff.'

Rather shyly she said, 'I should like to hear about your work in India some time. Your father is very proud of what you are doing on the missions there. He used to read us excerpts from some of your letters. It all sounds very exciting.'

Tom Hunter made a derisory snorting sound.

'Exciting? My dear girl, it was all dirt, disease and death, and sheer bloody hard work in rotten conditions.'

She was surprised by his vehemence. His letters, while not romanticising the situation, had always sounded full of hope and admiration for the people he was working for and with. He sounded now as if he had hated every minute of his time in India and the Far East.

He noted her reaction and ventured an apology of sorts. 'It wasn't, of course, all bad; far from it. But it is amazing that, with all the publicity on television and in magazines showing how lousy it is, a lot of people here seem to think of it in terms of adventure, *Boy's Own* variety.'

She said stiffly, 'I assure you, Dr Hunter, I'm not one of them.' She turned to the bed chart that almost filled one wall. 'Shall we make a start on this?'

'That's what I'm here for, Sister, to familiarise myself with the situation.'

He sounded as stiff as she did, but, as time went on and they got involved in a discussion about beds and patients, they began to relax. They were both dedicated professionals, and even if their personal introduction had got off to a shaky start there was no doubt that within half an hour they were each aware of the other's working qualities.

Just as they were about to go on their tour of the wards, Jacky Walsh appeared in Clare's office.

Clare performed introductions. 'Sister Jacky Walsh, admin sister, Dr Tom Hunter.'

Dr Hunter's eyes didn't exactly come out on stalks, but he took a good, hard second look at Jacky with her red-brown hair like a flaming bush topped by the starched frilly cap of a sister, the huge green eyes, faintly shadowed, wide generous mouth, modestly lip-sticked, and curves worthy of a page-three pin-up.

Clare was amused to see this contained-looking male as readily fascinated by her beautiful colleague as many a lesser man.

'For any of your needs, Doctor, don't hesitate to ask me. That's what I'm here for, from beds to scalpels, calling a meeting to booking a theatre. My brief covers supplies and a host of other things.' She flashed him a devastating smile.

'Well. . .' his deep voice seemed to take on yet a deeper tone '. . .that'll be an offer I can't refuse, Sister—to satisfy any of my needs.'

Jacky had perched herself on the corner of Clare's desk and now slid off. Had she noticed the innuendo in the doctor's voice? Clare wondered.

'Drop in any time; I'm just down the hall. I'll leave this for you, Clare.' She pushed a list across the desk. 'It's the equipment for the new wing. Bye, now!'

Tom Hunter cleared his throat. 'Shall we begin our tour, Sister?'

They started with Men's Surgical, a ten-bedded ward neatly divided into curtained cubicles. Six of the beds were occupied; the other four would fill tomorrow for 'take in' and operations the following day.

'Mr Sorrell comes over to operate once a week,' explained Brian Ford, the charge nurse, 'bringing his team with him, and his registrar does a follow-up round the next day, then hands over to—well, actually, your father, normally.'

'I hope he'll hand over to me as normal in the future,' replied Tom, a smile taking the sting out of the slightly sarcastic tone of his reply.

They moved to Women's Surgical, a similar ward with a similar set-up. Clearly the sister and nursing staff were quite bowled over by the new doctor's obvious good looks. It was the same on the other wards, and Clare hoped that the advent of Tom Hunter wouldn't disturb the smooth running of the hospital. She could do without the added problems of inter-staff rivalry over an available male.

In the medical ward where Mrs Jackson and her stubborn ulcer resided, Clare, Dr Hunter and a simpering staff nurse were seen standing in the doorway by that lady.

'Oh, you've brought the doc, then, Sister, to look at my leg,' she called down the length of the ward.

'Be quiet! How dare you, Mrs Jackson?' hissed Staff Nurse before anyone else could speak.

'What's wrong?' asked the doctor mildly of Clare, giving the annoyed staff nurse a surprised look.

Clare explained about the ulcer. 'We've tried a couple of treatments since Mrs Jackson's been in, and she'd had several different things when still at home. I was going to ask you to look at it tomorrow.'

'If you or Staff don't object, Sister, I'll have a look now.'

They moved down the ward and stopped at Mrs Jackson's bed.

'May I have a look at your leg and the bothersome ulcer?' Dr Hunter asked the delighted patient.

'You sure can, Doc.'

Staff Nurse mumbled inarticulately and glared ferociously at Mrs Jackson as she drew aside the rug and carefully eased off the dressing, exposing the offending ulcer.

Dr Hunter squatted on his heels to examine the affected area better. 'What have we tried so far?'

Clare listed the various treatments, adding the names of creams that had been tried before Mrs Jackson had been admitted.

'Right; well, Mrs Jackson, we're going try an alternative treatment,' he explained. 'There's a foam-like dressing that comes already prepared to be fixed in place. It will treat the ulcer without anyone's having to touch it for a few days. That's important because the ulcer has a chance to heal without being disturbed. It assists nature to do her job of healing.'

'Sounds like magic.'

'Well, not quite, but it is one of the latest things on the market and I think it might be the answer for your particular problem. We'll probably have to wait to start till tomorrow, as this may not be in stock. But I believe it will be worth waiting for.'

'You're the doc!'

'So I am.' He pretended to sound surprised, and Mrs Jackson laughed uproariously at the mild joke.

'You're as bad as Sister, 'ere,' she said. 'Always good for a laugh, she is.'

Ridiculously, Clare felt herself blushing.

'I'm glad to hear it; a sense of humour is always important, and in our work essential.' He gave a quick glance towards the staff nurse, and Clare wondered if that young lady was listening and might take note. She was a good nurse in many ways, but patient-communication was not her best point.

They finished looking round at last, ending up in the three-bedded maternity unit, at present empty.

Dr Hunter was suitably impressed with the small but beautifully equipped wing. There was an examination and separate delivery-room on one side of the corridor, and a tiny nursery and the three-bedded ward on the other.

'All the mums are admitted under the care of their own midwives, who come in when called, when presentation is at sixteen centimetres. We have two resident midwives, and the obstetrician and paediatrician from St Johns are alerted.'

'A co-operative effort.'

'Exactly; we rather pride ourselves on our teamwork here at the Cottage Hospital, and much of the credit must go to your father and his efforts.'

He was unstinting in his praise. 'Good old Dad—he was always great with people. It's what made him such a super GP.'

'You didn't feel like following in his footsteps into general practice?'

'Like all young men, I was looking for bigger worlds to conquer. But at the end of the day?' His voice ended in a question mark.

Clare didn't know quite how to continue. Did he want to say more, she wondered, or was he communing more with himself? She ducked the various possibilities.

'Is there anything else you want to see, or discuss?' she asked. 'And would you like a cup of coffee?'

He answered no to both questions, and suddenly seemed anxious to be gone. He snatched his mac from the chair when they returned to the office, thanked her for her help and strode away down the corridor without a backward glance.

'Well, I wonder what brought that on,' Clare asked herself, settling at her desk to finish the evening's work. She decided that he was an excellent doctor with the patients, if his session with Mrs Jackson was anything to go by, but possibly a bit prickly as a colleague. Perhaps his time in the Far East, and the recent illness that had brought him home and made him available to relieve his father, had affected his temper. Only time would tell.

CHAPTER TWO

Tom called in at Clare's office quite early the next morning, before going off to do proper rounds. He was wearing a blue and white striped shirt and blue tie, and carrying a pale blue jacket which matched the smooth cotton trousers.

'Will I do?' he asked rather endearingly.

Clare was surprised. She hadn't thought him capable of uncertainty. 'Very nicely, very neat and proper.'

He groaned. 'It's so long since I had to dress up for a ward round I'd almost forgotten what was acceptable and what was not.'

'Your father, being of the old school, always wore suits and ties, but nowadays some of the younger doctors are less sartorially elegant.'

'Thank God for that. The weather man says that it's going to be a scorcher; I don't think I can stand a tie for too long.' He grinned nicely.

'You'll soon get into the way of things. Do remember that we are an independent hospital even though we do a lot of National Health work. We more or less make our own rules as long as they don't cross any rules laid down by our foundress.'

'Ah, yes, the famous duchess who put up the cash for the Cottage Hospital. Quite a lady, by all accounts. I must read up about her in order not to offend anyone while I'm acting MO.'

'You do that. Meanwhile, Doctor, if you're ready I'll take you to Men's Surgical and hand you over to Brian for your round. Presumably you will want to follow your father's routine until you've settled in.' Tom

15

nodded. 'In that case, start on the two surgical wards, and then go on to the medical and long-stay wards; discuss any cases with the sisters or charge nurses. Maternity's still empty, though two mums are expected in later today.'

Did she imagine it, or had an expression almost of distaste crossed his face at the mention of Maternity? Of course not—all doctors enjoyed delivering babies, not that he would be called upon to do that often. The midwives were all top-grade nurses, qualified to do stitching and give various injections not permissable to lesser grades. The MO held very much a watching brief. Though old Dr Hunger enjoyed being present at births, and the midwives, knowing this, often informed him when one was imminent, following the purely ethical message that a new mum had been admitted.

'Renews my faith in human nature, Clare,' he often said, 'seeing this recurring miracle.'

Somehow, she didn't think that his son shared his delight in new births.

'And after the round?' he asked.

'You come back here for a coffee and to further discuss any problems or changes that you think I should know about, or can help resolve.'

'Right; I'm ready when you are, Sister.'

'White-coat time,' said Clare, grinning and handing him a stiff linen coat from behind the door.

He groaned. 'Do I have to?'

'One of the rules.'

He shrugged himself into the coat, and immediately looked stunning. A film-star doctor, Clare thought, with a stethoscope rammed into a pocket and the starched whiteness making a foil for his tanned skin. She sighed; she could see problems ahead with half the staff and all the female patients falling for him hook, line and sinker.

She escorted him to Men's Surgical and handed him over to the charge nurse there. At least he should be safe in that ward.

It was a long time before Tom returned. Obviously this first round would take longer than any in the future as he had to get to know patients, case histories and staff.

He looked predictably tired upon his return. Clare thought that it was probably more on account of the formality of coat and occasion than volume of work. Then, recalling his recent severe illness, she wondered if in fact the sheer physical effort of visiting the wards might have affected him.

'Wow, I'm bushed,' he said, slumping in a chair. 'What a wimp, ambling round a few wards and being exhausted.'

'You only travelled back from the East a few days ago,' Clare reminded him bracingly. 'Anyone in the best of health would still be feeling a bit below par under the circumstances, and, Dr Hunter, you are not in top-notch condition, are you?'

'Right again, Sister,' he acknowledged with a wry grin. 'As Dad said, you nearly always are.'

'How do you like your coffee?' For some reason she didn't want to dwell on his father's references to her professional abilities.

'On this occasion, white, please, and plenty of sugar.'

Clare handed him a creamy cupful of sweet coffee, and pressed biscuits on him.

'That's better,' he said after a few minutes spent sipping and munching while she got on quietly with some paperwork. 'What a restful person you are, Clare.' He smiled and she returned his smile.

'When you're ready we'll discuss any points you want

to raise.' She felt the need to keep this feeling of drowning when he smiled at her under control, and what better way than to get on with work?

He said almost apologetically, 'There's rather a number, I'm afraid.' He took a notebook from his pocket and opened it. 'May I start with Women's Medical, even though it's not in order of the round?'

'Of course; wherever you like.'

Clare felt a sinking feeling in the pit of her stomach. She had a feeling that Staff Nurse Jones was going to come under attack, probably with justification. What a pity that Sister Hayward was still on holiday and, because Matron was off sick, she herself had not been able to act as relief sister. Old Dr Hunter understood, but Clare had a feeling that his son was not going to be so conciliatory.

'Staff Nurse Jones?' he said, a question in his voice.

'A very good nurse, knows her stuff, utterly reliable to give treatments and so on. Why?'

'I think you know why, Sister.'

'Yes,' Clare couldn't prevent the frustration creeping into her voice, 'her manner with patients leaves a lot to be desired. She has been told; she seems to have a blind spot.'

'Totally blind. I'm surprised that half those women don't throw something at her.'

'Well, they don't because most of them have been very ill and they know that, in spite of her unfortunate manner, they can trust her in an emergency. You should see her under pressure; she's good.'

'I'll take your word for that, but I hope I never have to: her day-to-day behaviour is a disaster as far as I'm concerned. That little Miss Jacobs, the PMT patient, will be driven to something foolish if left in that woman's care any longer. I mean it, Sister: I want one of them moved stat.'

Clare had expected a complaint, but had not considered such a definite command. She kept her composure, studying the doctor with her fine grey eyes while assessing what he had said. Should she accept his words at face value or talk him out of so precipitous an order? She decided that he meant every word and that argument would not only be useless but reduce her own authority. Much better to concede gracefully and remedy the situation.

'Yes,' she agreed, and saw a flicker of surprise cross his face. 'Something must be done about Miss Jacobs. I'll have a word with Di Thorpe—you met her; she's the sister on Women's Surgical. There's a side-ward empty. I'm sure that she and her staff will do all they can for Miss Jacobs, though you will appreciate that they are not geared for medical cases.'

'Anyone's better geared than that staff nurse.'

'You do dislike her, don't you?' remarked Clare.

'Yes, I do,' he said baldly. 'And I might yet have to think of reporting her to her surperiors. I understand she is seconded from the general hospital.'

Privately Clare wondered why in such a short while he should have conceived such a strong emotion about the girl. After all, she'd been suitably deferential to him when they'd visited the ward yesterday. Her faults were never in the line of rudeness to her superiors; almost, in fact, the reverse. What did he see in her that was so repugnant?

Why such a violent reaction? She wasn't the only nurse or even staff nurse on the ward, simply the senior at this moment in time. Surprising that he couldn't accept that.

They moved on to other points on his list. All quite sensible and acceptable and purely medical, with no personal overtones.

It was after midday when Tom left. 'Sorry to have

taken so long,' he apologised. 'It won't happen again. And thanks for acting so promptly over that young girl; I hope that I haven't stirred up a hornets' nest, but it seemed important to me.'

'Glad to have helped.'

'Dad should have arrived in Inverness long since,' he said, exchanging his white coat for his blue jacket. 'He was due to leave on time when we got to Gatwick.'

'Did you take him up there this morning?'

'Of course. It was a lovely run through the Sussex and Surrey countryside. Something I've missed over the last few years—the peculiar delicacy of an English summer morning. There's nothing like it anywhere else in the world.'

'No wonder you were exhausted after the round; you must have got up at the crack of dawn to drive to Gatwick and back.'

'Reasonably early. Now I'm off; if wanted, down at the Castle Arms, having a pie and a pint.'

'Enjoy it.'

'Oh, I will, Sister; that's another thing that one doesn't get anywhere else in the world—a decent pint of real ale.' He grinned and took himself off with long strides down the corridor.

How well his name suits him, thought Clare, listening to his receding footsteps. He looks and sounds like a hunter, all lean and ready to spring when necessary, just as he did on poor Jones. The four-legged variety of hunter, with tooth and claw barely sheathed. She's definitely had it where he's concerned; I suppose that I'd better have a word with the girl.

She did that later in the afternoon, having arranged for the transfer of Miss Jacobs to the surgical side-ward, and explaining to Jones why it was necessary.

The girl broke down trying to explain away her

rudeness to patients in general and this patient in particular because she didn't consider her genuinely ill.

'Why, for heaven's sake?' asked a puzzled Clare. 'Why is it you can be such a super nurse in an emergency or when someone is at death's door, and hopelessly indifferent when they are recovering?'

Jones sat mutinously silent except for a pathetic sniff now and again.

'Do you think people don't deserve nursing once they are out of danger?'

Jones shook her head.

Summoning up all her patience, Clare said gently, 'Look, my dear, I really want to help; is there anything you want to tell me?'

The floodgates opened. . .suddenly it was all pouring out. Jones loved theatre work, had taken her first staffing post in Theatre and had fallen foul within a few days of a bad-tempered surgeon. He had floored her with a few badly chosen words at a time when her normal calm was at its lowest, and she had slunk out of Theatre vowing never to return.

'It was just before my period, you see, Sister. I was feeling awful, a kind of PMT I suppose, although I don't like to think so. I think we should be able to rise above things like that, don't you?' She sounded incredibly pathetic.

'Whatever gave you that idea, Nurse? PMT is as real and as much a medical problem as asthma or migraine. It's a chemistry upset that can respond to treatment. Oh, my dear girl, what a rod you've made for yourself.'

It explained so much, of course: her general off-putting behaviour with patients she considered well enough to fend for themselves, and her particular antipathy to Miss Jacobs.

Clare got her to agree to see her GP and discuss her problem with him. Rather tentatively she asked the staff nurse if she might explain the situation to Dr Hunter.

'You see, Staff, if he understands why you were so rude to his patient he won't pursue the matter; in fact, I'm positive that he will be very understanding and not carry this any further. Otherwise he may feel compelled to speak to your senior nursing officer at the Royal.'

Either this threat of Clare's obvious desire to help encouraged Staff Nurse Jones to agree to Dr Hunter's being put into the picture. 'Though I don't know how I'll be able to look him in the face again,' she added after giving her consent.

'Don't be silly, Nurse—he's a doctor, and will treat the information as confidential. He won't be embarrassed and neither should you be. Now go off duty and make that appointment to see your own doctor.'

'Yes, Sister.'

Clare sat and thought about the situation for a few minutes, then lifted the phone and dialled the Doctors' Lodge.

'Tom Hunter,' said a deep voice in her ear almost immediately.

'I'd like to talk to you, please, if possible when off duty and off the premises.'

'That sounds promising.'

She could hear the smile in his voice. 'Sorry to disappoint you—it's business, but better discussed away from the hospital where we will almost certainly be interrupted. Besides, I'm due off duty but don't want to delay what I have to tell you.'

'I'm grateful for any reason that allows me to ask you out for dinner.'

'Thank you; what time?'

'I'll pick you up at seven-thirty, all right?'

'Fine.'

* * *

Clare changed into a daffodil-yellow cotton dress with a scooped-out neckline, fitted bodice and full skirt, and was just ready when Tom arrived at the flat's door. Everything had conspired to hold her up before coming off duty, and, instead of the long soak in a warm bath that she had planned, she'd had a quick shower and shampooed her hair in minutes, in order to be on time.

Apparently the finished effect was satisfactory, for he said immediately she opened the door, 'You look stunning; almost edible, like a lemon-cream puff.'

'Do I take that as a compliment?'

'You certainly should do—it's meant as one. How extraordinary. . .' he put out a hand and touched her short shining mop of corn-coloured hair '. . .one would think that the bright yellow of your dress would kill it, but it doesn't.'

He seemed genuinely intrigued by the effect, something that most men would not have noticed.

'You sound as if you understand about colour,' she said rather shyly, thinking how little she knew about this man.

'I paint a little; colours interest me.' He sounded gruff and as if he didn't want to pursue the matter further. He put a hand under her arm and steered her out towards his car. 'I thought we'd drive out of town and eat at the Carvery in Pethurst.'

'Lovely; they're frightfully expensive, you know.'

'I think I can manage a suitable splash for my first dinner in England with a girl for years.' He produced one of his devastating smiles.

'That's nice of you, especially as I more or less invited myself.'

'Think nothing of it.'

They drove out under the shadow of the castle into the open countryside behind the South Downs. The sun was still high in the western sky, which remained the cloudless blue that it had been all day.

They talked of all manner of things as they sped through the green and gold countryside. Lightweight, meaningless small talk which Clare found soothing. It occurred to her that it had been a long time since she'd been out with a man with whom she felt at ease. Usually she was fending off unwanted empty compliments, or more overt physical overtures of admiration.

The Carvery was an old Tudor house tucked into a strip of woodland just off the busy main road. It had a good reputation for both food and service. They were not disappointed. The menu was vast, as was the wine list presented to Tom, which he scanned indifferently.

'Would you mind very much if we stuck to a good champagne?' he asked Clare. 'I know that I can cope with that; I'm not sure about some of the better wines. Anyway, it would be sacrilege to drink them with less than complete enthusiasm.'

Clare, who knew little about wine, thought that champagne sounded marvellous and said so. Tom went into a bit of a huddle with the wine waiter, who seemed impressed by his knowledge and his reasons for choosing champagne.

From the menu Clare chose whitebait for starters, in the chef's special sauce, and guinea-fowl poached in wine, served on a bed of asparagus with sauté potatoes and minted peas.

Rather apologetically, Tom, choosing a large, medium rare steak, explained, 'I'm not really a red-meat fan, but I'm prescribing it for myself tonight for medicinal purposes.'

Clare made a suitable response and wondered just how ill he had been and perhaps still was.

'Now,' he asked when the waiter left them with their chilled champagne and starters. 'Do you want to talk through this problem while we eat, or would you rather wait till we're on the coffee stage?'

'Oh, now, I think; I shall probably lose my nerve if I wait any longer.'

'Nerve, Miss Browning? I thought you had an infinite supply of nerve.' He smiled to show that he was teasing, but there was something in his tone that made her think that he believed that she was a sort of iron lady of nursing.

'I'm just a simple, hard-working nursing sister, Dr Hunter, not a paragon of any sort.'

'Not what I've heard, or seen in the couple of days that I've been here. Hell of a responsibility running even a small hospital as efficiently as you seem to do.'

'It's purely accidental that I'm doing so. No one ever intended that I should play acting matron except to cover Miss Stone's days off and a fortnight's leave. Filling in for her for months, while she recovers from a fractured femur, was not on anyone's agenda, either the board's or mine.'

'My father's on the board. He reckons you're brilliant. According to him, you not only stepped into the breach without turning a hair, but have continued to play your role superbly.'

Clare was embarrassed, and wondered why he was making such a thing of it. He didn't seem like the sort of man to chuck praise around indiscriminately.

He was very perceptive, she discovered, for before she could speak he leaned across the table and patted her hand gently, saying, 'Sorry about that. Must sound a bit fulsome. I suppose it's by way of being an apology after making waves today about the Jones girl. You've enough on your plate without me barging in and making life more difficult. I shouldn't have thrown my weight about quite so dramatically on my first working day.'

'Oh, but you should. You were quite right to bring it to my attention and force me to do something. In the event, and that's what I wanted to talk to you about, I think Staff Nurse Jones will benefit from what's happened.' She proceeded to tell him the story of the staff nurse and her thwarted hopes of a career in Theatre, and the reason why she had retaliated by being beastly to Miss Jacobs.

They talked of mundane things for a few minutes while the waiters removed plates and served their main course. When they were alone again, Tom said in a quiet, gentle voice full of compassion, 'The poor girl, frustrated at every turn and all for the want of a little medical advice. Extraordinary that even nurses seem unwilling to do anything about this problem. Why do you think that is?'

'Because nurses are women first. Many grow up with a whole host of taboos like any other women, even in this day and age—you'd be surprised—and many feel that anything to do with their reproductive system has to be endured.'

'How very Biblical——' he sounded faintly sarcastic '—and I've been trying to persuade Indian women to turn their backs on ancient customs where their health or that of their families is concerned, sometimes, believe it or not, with success. It seems that I might as well have stayed at home and worked in Barnsley or Brighton, educating the female populations of those worthy towns.'

Clare felt a bit out of her depth. This man's mood could change dramatically in seconds. What had happened to him in the exotic, dirty, poor and sometimes starving Far East to produce this reaction? He seemed all at once bitter and discouraged, his fine lean face scored with tired lines, the brilliant blue eyes sombre. If only old Dr Hunter were here—he'd get to the bottom of it. Of course, if he were here his son wouldn't be, at least not in a professional capacity at the Cottage Hospital.

All at once she felt uncomfortable, even unreal, in the luxurious, typically Home-Counties-style restaurant. She wondered if perhaps the wealthy, supremely comfortable surroundings had reminded Tom of the poverty he had left behind in India. Perhaps that was contributing to his sudden bitter, sad reaction.

'Shall we go home?' she asked gently.

'Home?' he repeated bleakly as if he didn't understand quite what she had said.

'Back to the hospital. We've both got to make an early start in the morning.'

'Ah, yes, Theatre day. The gods in their greens arrive.'

'You don't like consultant surgeons?' She tried to sound light and amusing.

He answered wearily. 'They have their place in the scheme of things.' He lifted a finger and a hovering waiter appeared with the bill.

Clare was impressed with the neat, speedy way her companion settled the account. Many an escort, she'd found, made a production out of this simple procedure, as if airing some special male, but hitherto secret knowledge.

They drove back through a counstryside drenched in moonlight, and Tom seemed to relax as they toured along at a steady forty miles an hour.

'Lovely,' he said once, and then was silent again.

Clare agreed, and thought, What a waste of a beautiful night, sitting silently beside a very masculine and handsome man with apparently no thought of romance in his head. Remembering the many occasions when she'd had to fight off the unwelcome attentions of an escort, she was cross with herself for wishing things other than they were.

She and Tom had spent the sort of evening that she'd often wished possible, as friendly companions discussing work without any sexist overtones. And, considering the subject matter of their conversation—premenstrual tension—that was something of an achievement. At no time had Tom shown anything but a deep compassion for women afflicted with this problem. There'd been no hint of male supremacy, only a desire to help such patients and a justified anger that, because of their own lack of response, many women suffered unnecessarily.

He said suddenly, 'Sorry, I'm not being much of a host. Would you like to stop in the town for another drink or coffee?'

'No, thanks; I had a lovely meal and loads of champagne. I couldn't eat or drink another thing.'

They were forced to slow down to a crawl a few hundred yards from the wrought-iron gates of the hospital to avoid running into a car creeping along in front of them.

'Looks as if that car's had a bump in the rear; no wonder they're going at a snail's pace. Wonder if the driver is OK?'

Clare had a sudden premonition. The fuzzy outline of a head in the passenger-seat looked vaguely familiar.

'I believe it's one of the new mums due in today,' she said. 'She's been in several times to look round and familiarise herself with the layout.'

The car crept through the gateway and Clare and Tom followed.

'That poor woman could be in dead trouble if she had a whiplash from the bump. Not an ideal way to go into labour.'

He drew up behind the vehicle, which had stopped

cautiously in front of the main entrance. A midwife and porter, obviously already alerted about their arrival, came down the steps to meet them.

Tom leapt out of the car and was at the patient's door in seconds.

'Don't move,' he instructed the young woman in the passenger-seat. 'Tell me, have you had a bump on the way here, and did you suffer a whiplash or anything similar?'

The woman realised that he was a doctor. 'Yes, I feel a bit sick, Doctor, and my neck hurts.' She looked past him to where the resident midwife, Celia Field, was standing. 'Oh, Sister,' she said tearfully, 'Will my baby be all right?'

'I'm sure everything's going to be fine,' Celia said firmly. 'As soon as we get you inside we'll have a look to see how things are going.' She looked across at Clare, who was standing on the other side of the car. What happened? she mouthed over Tom Hunter's bent back, obviously not being fully in the picture. Clare explained.

'Oh, what a shame, and Mrs Leach was so looking forward to a natural delivery. That mightn't be possible now.'

Tom Hunter straightened up. 'I want a surgical collar before we move this lady,' he said briskly to no one in particular.

Clare heard herself say, 'Yes, Doctor,' in a properly subdued tone, and took herself off to the physiotherapy department to seek out the necessary piece of equipment. It took her only a few moments to collect two or three collars to ensure that they chose the most suitable.

Back at the car, Tom was explaining to the young couple what might have happened when the other car ran into them.

'Fortunately, and very sensibly, in spite of this,' he patted Mrs Leach's bulging abdomen, 'you were wearing a seatbelt.'

'That's David's doing, Doctor; he had it specially lengthened so that I could still use it.'

'Sensible chap.' Tom flashed a smile at the anxious husband, and another to his wife. 'It's almost certainly saved you from a true whiplash injury; that and the fact that the other car was going fairly slowly and you were accelerating away. But you've sustained a neck or possibly back injury of some sort, and we must protect you and the birth of your baby.'

Clare said, 'Doctor, I don't know which of these will be most suitable.' She showed him the three different collars.

'We'll try this one.' He took the simplest support collar from her and very gently eased it round Mrs Leach's neck.

At once she said, 'That feels marvellous.'

'We won't really know how effective it is till you stand, and then sit in the wheelchair,' Tom warned. 'Now swing your legs round, keeping your back as straight as possible.'

Mary Leach was a wonderful patient. She did exactly as he requested, and in a few minutes was installed in the chair and being wheeled towards Maternity.

CHAPTER THREE

JONATHAN JAMES LEACH was born at ten-twenty the following morning. He weighed three point two three three kilos, and his mother experienced the natural birth that she had so desired, in spite of a stiff neck and surgical collar. Tom Hunter stayed with her throughout the night.

'I'll take care of this end if you do the necessary down there,' he said jokingly, stationing himself at Mary's head, and thereby endearing himself to the midwives for keeps.

He came to report to Clare mid-morning that all was well. There was no hint of the distaste for the birth process that she'd suspected the previous day. He looked tired but elated, much as his father might have done.

'A nice little baby,' he told her. 'All the right number of fingers and toes, and bright as a button. Just, in fact, what his brave mother deserves.'

Clare was as pleased for him as for the Leaches. Although he'd said nothing to indicate his feelings, she felt that he'd surmounted some sort of private hurdle by being involved with Jonathan's birth.

'I'm glad everything worked out all right; it might have gone terribly wrong, Mrs Leach having had that accident when she did.'

Tom looked thoughtful. 'Just shows what a tighrope life is, doesn't it?' He gave her a lopsided smile that turned her stomach over. 'I'm off to have a shower, my dear Sister Browning, if that's OK by you. I shall then return, refreshed and ready for the theatrical fray, as it were.'

He sketched a salute of sorts and disappeared through the door of her office. She wasn't sure if he was being sarcastic or simply amusing about the fact that it was operation day. As far as she knew, he'd not yet met Mr Sorrell, the surgeon, or his registrar. Privately Clare thought that both men were rather conceited and full of themselves. In the event of a confrontation she wondered who might come off worst.

'Let's just pray that it doesn't happen,' she said to her office, and shivered.

Operations today were to begin at midday. She did a round as always, prior to pre-medication being given, to reassure each patient due to go to Theatre. Most of them had already been reassured by the ward sister or charge nurse, but she knew from experience that the more professionals who called in to have a word, the more it was appreciated by the patients. It helped to have visitors, as a patient had once told her—filled in the time waiting to go down, the most nerve-racking time. For, however familiar the procedure was to the surgeon and other staff, to each individual patient it was an ordeal that had to be faced.

She spent more time than she meant to with Miss Cooper, an elderly lady with no relatives near by and a few friends of her own age who found visiting difficult. This lady was due to have a cholecystectomy, but Mr Sorrell had hinted that there might be something more sinister that he would have to remove, as well as her gall bladder.

He'd only made vague noises to the patient, leaving it to the ward sister and his registrar to explain to her the possibilities. Clare had been involved as she had come in to do a round when Di Thorpe, rather reluctantly assisted by the registrar, was trying to explain to Miss Cooper what might happen.

Nobody wanted to frighten the lady, but she had to be told what to expect in case further and more complicated surgery might be necessary. The registrar wasn't much help, humming and hawing about surgeons always taking the opportunity to look for any other problems once a patient was in theatre.

Di had taken over. 'Miss Cooper,' she said gently, 'do you remember that Mr Sorrell said that he was a bit concerned about your pancreas perhaps being damaged because your gall bladder wasn't working properly?'

Reluctantly the patient nodded.

'Well, it makes sense for him to check this out while you are under anaesthetic. If there is anything to be done he will deal with it immediately.'

At this point Clare joined in. 'I know that I would jolly well have two for the price of one, Miss Cooper; just think, you wouldn't have to steel yourself for a second operation.'

'But won't it mean that I shall be down in Theatre for hours, and won't it take me much longer to recover?'

'Not necessarily——' it was difficult to explain to a layman that, once the first incision was made, it was as easy for the surgeon to do a long or short operation, the only proviso being that the anaesthetist was happy with the patient's condition '—and certainly not as long as preparing for a second op, should this be necessary. Mr Sorrell's a fine surgeon; he'll do exactly and only what's necessary. Trust him.'

Miss Cooper looked suddenly weary. 'I trust you, Sister,' she whispered, 'and Sister Thorpe. I'll accept what you say.' She gave them a tired smile and turned her face away.

The registrar had bridled a bit, obviously annoyed at not having secured the patient's confidence personally, but he had been relieved that the session was over, and had soon gone away.

Clare saw everybody else on the list before returning to her office. It was half-past eleven. Any minute now Mr Sorrell would arrive and expect coffee and a chat in her office before going down to Theatre. She didn't look forward to these occasions. The surgeon was either too patronising or too familiar.

'I bet he's a groper, given half the chance,' was Jacky Walsh's opinion.

When Mr Sorrell arrived a few minutes later he was accompanied by Tom Hunter.

'Met our new acting MO at the door, Sister. Thought he might join us for a coffee.'

'Of course, sir; I'll fetch another cup.'

It was always cups and saucers for the consultant surgeon—he had an aversion to mugs.

'Shall I get it?' asked Tom, backing towards the door.

'No!' boomed Mr Sorrell as if he'd suggested something indecent. 'Sister will be only too pleased to fetch it, won't you, Sister?'

Clare said that of course she was, and waited till she left the room before grinding her nice even white teeth. 'Disgusting man,' she muttered, collecting a cup and saucer from the ward kitchen.

Back in her office she found both men in deep discussion about the afternoon's surgery. She poured the coffee and sat quietly, ready to join in the conversation if required. Tom inclined his head as she placed his cup before him, but Mr Sorrell ignored her, obviously hell-bent on playing the role of a senior consultant for the benefit of the new man.

They went away presently, Mr Sorrell inviting Tom to join him in Theatre, an invitation which was accepted with alacrity. To Clare, both men's attitude was a surprise. It was a well-known fact that the surgeon preferred to have only his own team in Theatre with him, so his invitation to Tom was unusual, while Dr Hunter's tongue-in-cheek comment about surgeons didn't tally with his obvious pleasure in being asked to assist in Theatre.

For the second time in two days Clare found herself wondering at the man's motives and attitudes. Perhaps when she got to know him better, if ever, she would understand his contradictory attitudes.

In spite of her being very busy, the afternoon dragged. Clare, incurably honest, knew that it was because Tom Hunter was tied up in Theatre and would not put in an unexpected appearance to lift her spirits. How ridiculous can you get? she told herself angrily; You only met the man the day before yesterday and it was the other staff you were worried about falling under his spell.

It isn't as if he's all sweetness and light, she argued with herself. He'd been pretty brisk at their first meeting, fiercely arrogant over Jones, and coolly authoritative over Mrs Leach. She had to admit, though, that all his demands were in the interest of patient care and not of the variety of male chauvinism that made Mr Sorrell so objectionable.

She worried away at the ever-present pile of paper-work for an hour or so, and then did an afternoon round of the medical and maternity wards. Two patients interested her particularly, and she admitted to herself that it was because they had been closely involved with Dr Hunter.

In the female surgical ward, which was busy with pre-op and post-operation patients, she asked Sister Thorpe's permission to visit the side-ward. It wasn't strictly necessary for her to seek the ward sister's permission, but Clare had learned from Matron the value of good staff-relations.

'Always,' Miss Stone had said, 'ask whoever is in charge if you may do a round. It results in oceans of goodwill, and assures them of their authority.'

It paid dividends now.

'I'd be glad if you will keep the Jacobs girl company for a bit,' muttered a busy Diana Thorpe. 'I feel that we've neglected her today.'

For the first time since Jenny Jacobs's admission to the Cottage Hospital Clare found her in a cheerful mood.

'Isn't Dr Hunter brilliant?' she said. 'I feel tons better since starting on this pill, and he's really dreamy. It does me good just to see him. And I like this ward— there's always something going on. It's like the High Street today, with trolleys whizzing up and down.'

Clare agreed, explaining that it was Theatre day. She thought it unlikely that the introduction of additional magnesium into Jenny's diet, via the pill, would have had time to be effective. It was more likely that rest and a generally improved diet, plus nursing care, were having an effect. Not that it mattered what was the cause of the improvement at this moment; it was nice to see the girl happy and taking an interest in things about her.

She stayed for a few more minutes before moving on to the maternity unit. There she was introduced to the baby Jonathan by his proud mother. Another patient bowled over by the charismatic Tom Hunter.

'I've agreed to stay for a few days, Sister,' said Mrs Leach. 'Dr Hunter thinks that it is wise on account of my neck, though the X-ray showed that there's no serious damage. Wasn't I lucky that he was there to stop me rushing out of the car and making matters worse?'

'You certainly were.'

To Clare's surprise, Mrs Leach then said, a cheeky smile hovering round her lips, 'I'm sorry if I spoilt your evening, Sister, after you and Dr Hunter had such a lovely time.'

Clare felt herself blushing and at a loss as to what to say. Fortunately a nurse came to the door at that moment with a message that she was wanted on the phone. As she went to the ward office she wondered what on earth Tom had said about their innocent evening together to make Mrs Leach smile so knowingly.

Of course, he'd spent the whole night at her bedside and had probably talked a lot of nonsense to keep her relaxed. It was just a surprise that he'd mentioned their outing to the patient at all. Yet another sign of his unorthodox behaviour, she decided.

She was tidying her desk and preparing to depart when he came into her office. His hair was damp from the shower that he'd obviously taken after Theatre. He looked, if it was possible, even more handsome than earlier, with his thick hair springing from his high forehead a veritable mane, lion-like, complementing her idea of him as a hunter.

'I thought I might be in time for a cup of tea,' he said plaintively. 'But you look as if you're packing up for the night.'

'I am, and I'm sure that Sister Wood in Theatre offered you tea or coffee when you'd finished the list. You can't be that desperate.'

'Thou shalt not live by cups of tea alone, Sister. It's decent company that I seek, as well as sustenance.'

'I should have thought that Mr Sorrell and Bob Cutler would have provided the company, and Sister Wood the tea.'

Tom Hunter made a rude face. 'God preserve me.'

Clare relented. 'Oh, well, I suppose a few more minutes won't make any difference. I'll put the kettle on.' She made for the ward kitchen and he followed her.

He stood leaning against the door, hands in his trouser pockets jingling some change. 'I'm not very happy about poor Miss Cooper,' he said after a moment's silence. 'Sorrell didn't do anything except the cholecystectomy and cholangiography, the results of which were fairly satisfactory. But I'm surprised that he didn't attempt a repair of her hiatus hernia. No way would I advise anyone to have that op if it could be avoided, but once on the spot as it were. . .' He shrugged and looked impatient, clearly irritated by the surgeon's caution. 'Poor old girl, I'm afraid that she won't be that much more comfortable after losing her gall bladder—the hernia's likely to play her up after being aggravated by the operation. We'll have to watch her closely, give her plenty of pain-killers and explain the problem to her.'

Clare was touched by his concern for Miss Cooper. It illustrated yet again his professional commitment, and she could sympathise with his impatience with Mr Sorrell's very orthodox and pedantic ways. He was a good surgeon but without imagination, and certainly without the flair that some surgeons exhibited. She supposed that Dr Tom Hunter would have plenty of that if he ever took up surgery. Perhaps he would pursue a surgeon's path, now he was back in Britain, rather than medicine. He was qualified to do so.

He carried the tray back to her office, where they drank the pot dry while he scoffed most of her biscuits. At first all the talk was of the cases he'd assisted with that afternoon, but presently the conversation grew more personal.

He said how much he had enjoyed their outing the previous evening, and hoped that they might repeat it.

'Some time perhaps,' said Clare, deliberately cautious. 'I might be going home for a couple of days at the end of the week.

'Where's home?' he wanted to know.

'Near Bath.'

'How near?'

'Just a few miles out of the city. A small village.'

'I ask,' he said in an amused voice, making a nonsense of her cautious replies, 'because I have friends at Tinnesly and I wondered if you lived anywhere near there.'

Feeling foolish, and reminding herself that he probably was not much interested in her private life and only asking out of politeness, she replied in a high voice, 'How strange—my people live in the next village, Tottering.'

'Pretty place; played tennis there, oh, must be all of ten years ago, at the rectory. My friends the Barlows knew the then rector rather well.'

Why she didn't at once say that the rector, then and now, was her father, she had no idea. But, the moment having passed, she found it impossible to explain that Bob and Tansy Barlow were known to her and still played tennis at the rectory on occasion.

She brought the conversation to an end as soon as she decently could, pleading a telephone call that she was expecting from abroad. This was halfway true, since her sister often phoned from Zurich in the middle of the week, but would not have been one whit disturbed had Clare not been there to take her call.

'Oh, well,' said Tom, 'thanks for the tea and most of all the company. I'd better tootle off and do another round of the post-ops. See you tomorrow.'

'Sure.'

Clare went off to her nice little flat in the sisters' home, feeling hot, cross and angry with herself. How on earth was she going to untangle the business of the Barlows? Of course, she tried to cheer herself with the thought, Tom might not be in touch with them for ages, if at all. Perhaps they were not such great friends; maybe he wouldn't contact them during his stay at the Cottage Hospital, and she was getting into a state for nothing.

Even as she pretended that this might be a possibility, she knew that it was false. He had spoken of his friends in a casual but affectionate manner, the way one does, she thought, about very old friends. He wouldn't pass up an opportunity of seeing them now that he was back in England. She tried to be philosophical about it, but the thought was still worrying her when she went to bed, causing her to toss and turn for much of the night.

CHAPTER FOUR

THE next few days were so busy that Clare had little time to worry about her silly reaction to Tom Hunter's reference to a long-ago tennis match.

Maternity had a rush of mums all suddenly coming to term and needing admission. Mrs Leach and baby Jonathan went home after two days, although ideally they should have stayed a little longer. Fortunately both mother and baby were doing extremely well, and neither seemed unduly affected by the slight accident that had occurred.

The Cottage Hospital didn't boast a casualty department—this was situated in the general hospital a few miles away—but an attached first-aid unit dealt with minor accidents. The unit was only open during the summer months from nine to six, expressly to treat visitors to the castle, though anybody who turned up with a minimal condition was treated. It was staffed by St John's and Red Cross members, with the trained staff from the hospital on call if necessary.

The weather continued to be hot and sunny. Proper holiday weather, bringing visitors to the castle from far and wide. There was a rush of patients with minor cuts, bruises and stings in the first-aid unit, and, one morning, two cases of mild food-poisoning.

Clare's phone rang.

'Tom Hunter here,' announced his deep rich voice in her ear. 'Is it possible to arrange admission for the day of two patients? They need fluids plus general nursing care. Holidaymakers, renting a houseboat on the river, enthusiastically scoffing local cockles fished

41

from the estuary. Not too many, thank God, and the worst is over. They'll be all right, given care and replacement of lost fluids for a few hours.'

'I'll ring you back. They should go to the general hospital; we don't usually admit from the unit.'

'But you'll try to accommodate them, yes?'

'I'll see what I can do.'

'Many thanks.'

It really wasn't too difficult to arrange. There was an empty side-ward on Men's Medical, and Sister Bacon was only too willing to put an extra bed in there for the day.

'Wouldn't miss the chance of having our Doctor Hunter popping in and out,' said that middle-aged, usually very down-to-earth lady to Clare.

'Oh, not you too!' muttered Clare to herself as she put down the phone. Everyone, it seemed, was crackers over the man.

She relayed the news to Dr Hunter, who was still in the first-aid unit.

'I knew you'd work a miracle. I'll bring them up in my car in a few minutes.'

He called in at her office half an hour later. 'Thanks for fixing up the White couple,' he said, giving her a heart-stopping smile. 'They'll be on their feet in no time, given Sister Bacon's brand of tender loving care. I bet she's already got a couple of pints of water into them.'

'Sister Bacon's a force to be reckoned with.'

'Like our beautiful deputy matron.'

His words and the warmth with which he said them made her cheeks grow warm. A fact which didn't escape him.

'How refreshing—a woman who can still blush.'

'Dr Hunter, if you're not busy, I am. Please leave me to get on with my work.'

'Giving me the brush-off, Clare?' He leaned across the desk and took her hands in his. His voice was even deeper and throatier than ever. 'Will you come out to dinner with me tonight?'

She shook her head, not trusting herself to speak, trying to control the trembling of her hands that he held imprisoned in his.

He said softly, 'You promised you would come out with me again. Please.'

There was a knock at the door which was opened almost at once to admit Jacky Walsh.

'Oh, sorry,' she said, grinning broadly and obviously not a bit sorry, seeing Clare trying to free her hands from the doctor's grasp.

'I'm trying to persuade Clare to have dinner with me,' said Tom coolly, not in the least perturbed by her entrance.

'I'm willing if Clare isn't,' Jacky announced cheerfully in her bold, uninhibited manner.

With all her heart Clare wished that she might be as easy with the doctor as Jacky. But that, she knew, was to wish herself a different person. Jacky was a splendid nurse, a beautiful woman, and a good friend, but her attitude to sex and men was a world away from Clare's. For, even these days, a country rectory unbringing left its mark.

Not that she felt any sense of superiority towards Jacky or other girls with a similar attutide to sex. In fact she occasionally envied them, even wished that she might emulate them in their freer ways. But somehow it wouldn't work for her, and, apart from a short relationship with a houseman at her training hospital, she had kept all her friendships light and untouched by sex or commitment.

Her attitude had earned her the label of being cold

and peculiar by some men who had thought an evening's outing earned them a bed for the night. They didn't ask her out again, which was a relief, but a few of her dates had understood, or tried to understand her attitude, and remained friendly. One or two of the more enlightened even admired her for sticking to her morals.

She wondered, watching Tom Hunter laughing with Jacky, which category he would fall into. He was so obviously sexy and used to bowling women over that he would probably have little patience with someone he considered full of old-fashioned hang-ups over sex. On the other hand, he was a responsible medical man, well aware of the hazards of over-indulgence, and might well be cautious on that account.

Jacky's voice cut in across her thoughts.

'Some of the furniture has arrived for the day-unit, Clare. I thought if you had time we might arrange it together.'

Clare thought that she saw a way to speed Dr Hunter on his way without further reference to the invitation to dinner.

'Right, give me a quarter of an hour to finish this paperwork and I'll be with you.' She turned to look at the doctor, who was sitting, very much at his ease, in the chair on the other side of her desk. He was regarding her with twinkling blue eyes as if reading her thoughts. 'You can see that I am very busy, Doctor.' She tried to avoid meeting his eyes. 'If you'll excuse me?' She picked up a pen and made an attempt to write.

Jacky said brightly, 'I'm away, then; see you presently, Clare.' She looked at Tom. 'Don't forget, if you're short of a dinner partner, I'm free.'

'I'll bear it in mind.'

Jacky left, and Clare ostentatiously continued writing until Tom put a hand over hers and stopped her.

'Come out with me tonight; I need to talk, and you're the most relaxing person I've met in years.'

Clare wasn't sure if she liked the description. It seemed to indicate that he wasn't expecting her to be more than a good listener. It occurred to her that this was perhaps what her own attitude to men indicated. You can't have it both ways, she told herself. A man who respects you *and* high romance.

He seemed to read her thoughts.

'No strings, Clare,' he said softly in his velvet-deep voice. 'Just a pleasant evening, talking shop or whatever you wish.'

'Will you go away and leave me to get on if I say yes?'

'Willingly.'

'Then yes, I'll come out tonight.'

'Thank you. I'll pick you up at seven, OK?'

'OK.'

He uncurled his long lean body from the chair, gave her another devastating smile, and left.

A few hours later Clare stood in her bedroom, trying to decide what to wear for the evening. She had no idea what sort of place Tom would choose for dinner. If his knowledgeable and experienced taste in wine and food were as worldly as they had appeared on their first date, the venue might be very sophisticated. On the other hand, they might go into the country for a pub meal.

She decided on a pair of newly acquired black crêpe, box-pleated culottes, cool, casual but also smart, and a pure silk raspberry-coloured shirt with delicate embroidery on the turned-back collar. The outfit should meet any occasion.

Tom Hunter obviously thought so when he arrived a few minutes after she'd completed her toilet.

Directly she opened the door he commented, 'Beautiful; so right.' His amazing blue eyes surveyed her coolly from top to bottom. She flushed beneath his gaze. 'Delightful,' he murmured. She felt like an innocent schoolgirl in spite of her sophisticated outfit.

He stepped into the room at her invitation, closed the door behind him, and leaned against it. He looked incredibly handsome and strong, the width of his shoulders enhanced by a pale linen jacket over a silk shirt and narrow black tie, which was looped into a loose knot and matched his black tapering-legged trousers.

The way that his dark hair, peppered with grey, sprang from his high, wide forehead, above straight black eyebrows, somehow accentuated his virility. A high-bridged aquiline nose over well-marked, but not full lips confirmed his sexuality. Those lips were curved now into an appreciative and provocative smile.

Clare, fascinated by the sheer masculine elegance of the man before her, thought that he was ready to kiss her at any moment. She both wanted and dreaded the moment's arriving.

He leaned forward and, like a conjuror, produced a spray of deliciously scented lilies of the valley from behind his back.

'To perfect perfection,' he said, smiling gently. 'Here, I think, don't you?' His fingers explored the area by the lapel of her shirt, just above her left breast. She used every ounce of self-control not to shiver at his touch.

He fished with long fingers in his jacket pocket and drew forth a small gold safety-pin.

'You are well prepared,' Clare managed to say in a shaky, husky voice.

'Like the good Boy Scout that I once was.'

He fastened the flowers to her blouse and the scent from the dainty waxen blooms wafted up between them.

'Oh, my dear,' he said in a thick, throaty murmur as he folded her in his arms.

He held her for a few moments, to her surprise not rushing to kiss her. A kiss for which she had steeled herself and determined to resist if it became too demanding.

He brushed the top of her hair with his lips and then stood her a little way from him and kissed her forehead. To her amazement, and a mixture of relief and chagrin, he only briefly touched her lips with his.

Astonishingly he said, still holding her, but lightly so that she could slip from his embrace if she so chose, 'It's too soon for you yet, isn't it? You are not as ready as other women to enjoy a bit of sex on the side, are you?'

Recovering from her surprise at his restraint and gentleness, she shook her head. She wondered how he could possibly know how she felt. Surely she wasn't as obvious as all that?

She recalled the words of a registrar with whom she'd had a brief unhappy friendship.

'You are a deceiver, looking,' he had complained, 'as if ready for anything, and pulling out at the last moment. It's women like you who get blokes into trouble,' he'd continued nastily, 'leading us on and then complaining when we want to do the obvious.'

She had made up her mind then that she would never knowingly present the wrong image, and she hadn't. She had always been honest with her escorts, letting them know at the outset of an evening together how she felt about one-night stands. Until now, and the perception exhibited by Tom Hunter, it was usually several hours before she was believed with varying degrees of good or bad humour.

But to have her sensibilities read and understood without a word from her was a unique experience. Coming from this man, who'd already caused her heart and senses to react sensationally to his presence, it was almost hurtful. She realised that she had wanted him to want her. To find him capable of withstanding her attractions and prepared to accept the barriers that she erected, out of his own intuition and strength, was difficult to accept.

She was almost at a loss how to handle the situation. He'd been kind and gentle, but perhaps he was already disappointed at the thought of the evening ahead.

'If you want to call dinner off,' she began tentatively, 'I shall quite understand.'

He looked at her in genuine astonishment. 'My dear girl, do you mean because you're not prepared to tumble into bed with me?' He threw back his head and gave a shout of laughter. 'Thank you for being so honest about it, but I assure you that companionship is a much harder commodity to come by than sex, and it's your company I want more than anything.'

'Oh, if you're sure.'

'Positive, Clare.' His blue eyes gleamed with laughter, and he shook her gently by the shoulders. 'Come on, let's get going; I'm starving—and I don't mean sex-starved.'

They had a marvellous evening. He drove out of town along the river road for several miles. The evening sun was beating a golden path across the sea as still as the proverbial mill-pond as they reached the estuary. He pulled off the road on to a tarmacked area in front of an old lighthouse, recently converted to a restaurant.

The meal was delicious. On the recommendation of

the waiter, they had avocados and limes chopped into a creamy sauce for starters, followed by a platter of deep-seafood.

'Don't want to emulate the Whites and end up in our own first-aid station,' said Tom, having confirmed that the dish was made up of fish caught well out to sea and not in the estuary.

'We won't, will we?' askeed Clare, momentarily alarmed.

'Of course not, love, as long as they are deep-sea fish.'

Clare savoured the mild endearment though she tried to be sensible, telling herself that people used words like 'love' without any deep meaning attached.

They finished their meal with a huge bowl of fresh raspberries and cream.

'Another very English dish,' said Tom, 'that I used to tease myself about on hot summer nights in India.'

Clare thought that he might be in a mood to tell her something of his travels, but directly they'd finished eating he suggested that they dance. When she agreed, he swept her on to the minute floor where they danced for a long while to the romantic music provided by the three-piece band.

It was a lovely way to end the evening, either locked together in old-fashioned waltzes, or moving sensuously in unison in few feet apart for the more modern pieces.

She would have liked the night to go on forever with the dancing an excuse to be close to him. The feel of his arms about her was wonderful. The rock-like strength of his chest and shoulders and the masculine smell of his aftershave sent shivers of excitement quivering down her spine.

Aware that if he demanded anything of her now she would give in, she pulled a little away from him.

'Tired, love?' he asked softly, bending his head to look into her eyes.

She didn't want the evening to end in spite of her tenuous state of mind. She shook her head. 'No, I could dance all night.'

'As the song says.'

'Yes.'

'And I; it's been a great evening; very special. Do you feel that too?'

'Oh, yes,' she breathed.

Some unknown time later the tiny orchestra struck up the music for the last dance, and soon after they left the Lighthouse to drive back through the warm, starry night.

They had driven a little way in a companionable silence when Tom said abruptly, 'I had a look at Mrs Jackson's ulcer today. The new treatment seems to be working. It's healing at last.'

His change of mood and conversation was like a douche of cold water. Clare, who had spent the last few hours wrapped not only in the arms of this handsome man, but in a glow of love and growing physical desire, drew in her breath sharply.

With a great effort she tried to match his seeming cool professionalism. 'Oh, that's splendid. I'm glad you checked; I thought it about time to see how things were going on.'

'Yes, it's a temptation, isn't it, to start fiddling with the dressing too soon, not knowing what's going on underneath?'

The moon was streaming across the sea, turning it to silver, just as the sun had earlier lit it with gold. The stars were huge, almost touchable. The lowered roof of the car allowed the soft scented air of the summer night to waft around them—and they were talking of varicose ulcers!

Clare felt slightly hysterical and had difficulty controlling a desire to giggle. Tom seemed unaware of her reaction.

'Will you come with me tomorrow when I have a look at Miss Cooper? I'm not happy about her recovery. Sister's off duty. It won't be stepping on the staff nurse's toes, will it, if you come on the round?'

He had obviously meant what he'd said the day after he arrived about being more careful of people's feelings.

Clare swallowed her hurt and disappointment at the way the evening had changed. He probably had his reasons for suddenly being impersonal and professional. After all, he had already accepted that there was nothing more to be expected than a goodnight kiss when they arrived home. He must be preparing himself for a petering out of the evening. He couldn't know that his presence and the magic of being held close by him might have changed her mind about a more intimate end to their evening together.

'No, Staff won't mind; I quite often do a round with the MO if Sister's away.'

'We must work out some medication to make that poor soul more comfortable. She's still vomiting more than she should be and consequently enduring considerable pain from her hiatus hernia. She badly needs reassuring and that's certainly your forte.'

They talked of various combinations of nausea and pain-control medication that might be given by injection or, while the patient was still on a drip, intravenously. Tom had tried several mixtures of drugs with varying degrees of success.

'What I would really like to come up with,' he said, looking remote as he concentrated, 'is something that Miss Cooper can continue with orally when she goes home. Something that she feels that she can rely on to see her through the next few weeks.'

Clare agreed. 'It would certainly give her confidence, as she lives on her own.'

'Pity she can't go somewhere to convalesce.'

'There's a niece in the West Country. She's coming to visit next week. Perhaps she would have her for a week or two.'

'What a good idea. Do you think we might tackle her together when she comes? See if we can persuade her to take her aunt for a holiday?'

'We can try, but I have an idea that Miss Cooper herself might be obstinate about going away.'

'Amazing how tough and determined frail old people can be when they've a mind. You'd think she'd jump at the chance.'

They turned in at the hospital gates, and he drove straight up to the sisters' flats. He stopped in front of her ground-floor rooms, and was out of the car and round to her side of the vehicle before she had undone her seatbelt.

'Key?' He held out his hand and she gave it to him without a word.

He unlocked her door and handed back the key.

Clare felt shy and unsure of herself. 'Would you like to come in for coffee?'

'I'd like to but I'm not going to, dear girl, for many good reasons, all of which you are aware of.'

He leaned against the door-jamb, watching her with his blue eyes almost concealed between half-closed lids.

'I've no intention of spoiling a lovely evening by jumping the gun. My intentions are honourable enough, but, my God, the flesh is weak.' He waved a hand at the star-studded sky. 'What a waste, to talk of hernias and ulcers on a night like this.'

'Yes,' Clare whispered. 'That's what I thought.'

'But definitely safer than too many of these.' He pulled her into his arms and kissed her hard and painfully on her parted lips. 'Now go to bed,' he said, pushing her through the door, 'and let me see you looking your beautiful, cool, professional self in the morning.'

He got back into the car and sped off down the drive.

The next morning was hectic. Diana Thorpe's boyfriend phoned to say that she had gone down with some sort of bug and wouldn't be on duty. With the sister on Medical off duty and a staff nurse short there, both Clare and Jacky Walsh had to step into the breach and each supervise a ward.

Clare took over Surgical as it was take-in day for the next day's operations and the staff were run off their feet. There was a competent senior staff nurse on duty, but an unsure junior and two new student nurses. Fortunately the middle-aged auxiliary nurse, who'd been on the ward for years, was as always worth her weight—which was considerable—in gold.

Clare was completing the admission details of a nervous young woman, booked for an appendicectomy the following day, when Tom arrived on the ward.

She heard his voice as he spoke to one of the nurses before he entered the office. Her heart thumped painfully, and she felt herself blushing at the remembrance of his fierce kiss and his words last evening. The girl sitting the other side of the desk looked at her with interest, for a moment forgetting her own problems. Clare felt ashamed of having betrayed herself by blushing.

When Tom came into the office the girl transferred her interest to him, her eyes widening with surprise and pleasure at the sight of such a handsome man. It was all too easy to read her thoughts, and Clare knew that her own were almost as obvious.

She avoided Tom's eyes and said very formally, 'Good morning, Doctor. I'm glad that you've come. I was just assuring Miss Kent here that there should be no problems with her operation tomorrow. She's being admitted for an appendicectomy.'

Miss Kent fluttered long dark eyelashes over baby-blue eyes. 'I'm so frightened, Doctor,' she said in a husky whisper. 'I've never been in hospital before.'

Tom gave her a long, gentle look. 'Has anybody come with you?' he asked, 'to see you safely installed?'

She shook her head. 'I haven't been living here long enough to make friends, and my parents live in Cornwall.'

'Where do you work?'

'In the bank in the High Street. They've been awfully good, considering that I've only just been transferred to them. I've been ill almost since I arrived.'

'Well, Miss Kent, we'll soon have you fit again to return to work. But you'll have to go back home for some convalescence after your operation. You're a lucky girl, having a home in beautiful Cornwall.'

The girl mumbled something, which Clare didn't catch, and said to Tom, 'You will be with me when I have my operation, Doctor, won't you? I shouldn't be so frightened if I knew you were going to be there.'

It was the most blatant piece of making up to a man that Clare had ever seen, but Tom seemed oblivious of this. All men are suckers, she thought, for a little-girl voice and a pair of China-blue eyes.

'I'll certainly be around,' he said, and gave her a reassuring pat on the shoulder.

Nice, motherly Nurse Rowntree put her head round

the door. Clare said thankfully, 'Will you show Miss Kent to her bed, Nurse, and help her settle in?'

Miss Kent followed her reluctantly from the office, batting her eyelids at Tom again as she left.

Surely, thought Clare, he will make some amused remark about the girl, show that he realises that she is just making a pass at him?

He did no such thing. 'Poor girl,' he said. 'What a rotten thing to have happened just after leaving home. She must feel very lonely.'

'The bank has a good reputation for staff care.' She couldn't stop her voice from sounding cool and reserved.

Tom looked at her in surprise. 'She's very young to be ill and away from home. She's frightened too. We must do all we can to reassure her.'

'Well, naturally; it's my job. I can assure you that she will have every care and attention.'

He gave her another surprised look and said evenly, 'I wouldn't expect anything less of you as a superb professional, but a little more warmth, perhaps, would not come amiss in this instance.'

It was unbelievable that he should criticise her handling of the girl. She had been doing all she could to reassure that young lady until he'd arrived and taken over, or been taken over by Miss Kent's acting the maiden in distress. Did he really think her capable of being hard or indifferent to a patient, *any* patient?

Clare decided not to pursue the matter. The last thing she wanted was to spoil the lovely relationship they had achieved last night. She would ignore his last remark.

'Do you want to see Miss Cooper?' she asked, producing a smile, and rising to find the patient's file in the cabinet.

He moved across the office and stood behind her.

He slipped his hands round her waist and pressed her to him, nuzzling the back of her neck as she stood with her head bent over the files.

She found it difficult to breathe.

'I do needle you, love, don't I?' He kissed the back of her neck. 'And I don't mean to. It's just that I want you to be perfect at all times, even to people like that little minx Cathy Kent.'

'So you did realise that she was putting on an act for you?'

'Well, if nothing else she was obvious, was she not? Though I think her nervousness about her op was genuine.'

'Oh, yes, poor little thing; I was trying to reassure her before you arrived.'

'Being the perfect nurse.' He turned her to face him. 'Given another time and place, I should like to make mad, passionate love to you.' He sounded very matter-of-fact. He kissed her forehead gently and stroked her cheek with his long index finger.

She couldn't decide whether he was being serious or facetious. He took the folder from her and opened the door. 'Time we went to see Miss Cooper, I think, don't you?' he asked, as if she had been delaying them.

She made an angry sound in her throat and preceded him from the office. So many changes of mood, she thought, in a few minutes, laced with criticism and admiration for my actions. What does he want of me?

Miss Cooper had just been sick again when they arrived at her bedside.

'I don't think that I can go on much longer,' she mumbled, looking pale and miserable.

'Sister and I have been giving your problem a lot of thought, Miss Cooper,' said Tom, giving Clare a lovely smile, reminding her of the pleasures of the previous evening. He sat down on the side of Miss Cooper's bed and, taking one thin hand in his, continued, 'We think we've come up with a combination of medicines that will stop this sickness, and take away much of your pain. It is going to be inserted through the drip here, so you won't feel anything, but it should begin to work in a short while.'

'You've decided, then, on the cimetidine, hourly over twenty-four hours?' asked Clare.

'Yes, together with metoclopramide hydrochlor per body weight. I'll work out the exact dose and we'll start it immediately.'

'Don't worry about the fancy names,' he reassured Miss Cooper. 'They are both medicines that you can have to take by mouth when you go home.' He smiled and moved to the end of the bed to calculate the amounts that she should have.

Clare asked a staff nurse to bring the medicines from the drug cupboard, and a few minutes later she was injecting the prescribed amount into the drip. Tom wrote up the patient's chart for future doses.

'You'd better supervise Miss Cooper's hourly injection, Staff,' Clare instructed the senior staff nurse, 'and when you're off duty I'll take over.'

'Yes, Sister.'

'I'll be back this afternoon, Sister, to check up on the admissions,' said Tom abruptly and strode away down the ward.

'I give up,' muttered Clare to herself, wondering at his sudden departure after his gentleness and the intimate smile he had exchanged with her moments before. 'The man's a mystery.'

'I beg your pardon, Sister?' said the puzzled staff nurse.

'Nothing, Staff; talking to myself,' she replied briskly. 'Now, about these other admissions.' She sailed across the ward, followed by her assistant. 'I'll help you make up these two beds.'

She kept herself busy for the rest of the morning, doing more than her fair share of the physical work of baths and dressings and other mundane chores. Somehow she didn't feel that she could sit in the office doing paperwork; her mind was too full of Doctor Hunter and his moods.

Most of the ward work completed, she and the staff nurse retired to the office for coffee.

'I see you're on a split today, Staff,' said Clare, glancing at the duty roster.

'For my sins,' Janet Wells replied, pulling a face. Nobody liked split duty.

'If it isn't too late to alter your arrangements I'd be happy to swap with you—I've something to attend to this afternoon.'

'Oh, Sister, that'd be super. I was only going to go window-shopping this afternoon. I'd rather meet my friend this evening.'

'Good, I'm glad; it'll help me out. Everything seems quiet now that the admissions are in. Dr Hunter will be in to examine this afternoon.'

'Another bonus,' said her colleague happily, rolling her eyes dramatically.

'Not you too, Staff!'

'Well, you've got to admit, Sister, he's rather dishy, and nice with it.'

'Hmm,' muttered Clare, but smiled, pleased with herself for having taken avoiding action for the afternoon. She convinced herself that the less she saw of him, the less he would intrude on her thoughts. She would soon regain the calm poise that she'd possessed before he'd arrived on the scene and ruffled it.

The afternoon was wasted. Clare sat in the garden under the shade of the trees, pretending to read. Tom

Hunter's face kept appearing between the pages. His voice, telling her last night that he wanted to stay for coffee but didn't dare, competed with the buzzing bees for her attention. He'd sounded so genuine, so honestly concerned for her and her beliefs. And this morning in the office, when he'd pinned her against the filing cabinet and kissed the back of her neck! Surely he'd meant what he said, explaining his 'needling' her because he wanted her to be perfect.

So why had he rushed off directly he'd finished attending to Miss Cooper? Why a sudden coolness in his voice and eyes? She racked her memory, trying to recall if anything, however small, had occurred in those few minutes to cause his displeasure. Nothing, nothing had happened except that he'd had a sudden change of mood. Well, she didn't want anything to do with a moody man, however handsome and, when he chose, silver-tongued.

Just before she went on duty the phone rang.

'Hi! Long time, no see,' said a voice in her ear.

'Bill! Bill Bennett! How are you? Where have you been for the last few months? Where are you now?'

'That's a lot of questions needing long answers, sweetie. It'll take hours to give you all the news. What about dinner tonight? I'll pick you up about seven.'

'Sorry, I'm on duty till eight, and then some—you know how it is.'

'A drink, then, and a pub snack about nineish; would that be OK?'

'Fine. Look, don't come for me, as I'm uncertain when I'll be ready. I'll meet you down at the Castle Arms.'

'Great, I look forward to that. We've a lot to talk about, sweetie.'

Walking back to the ward, Clare felt a great wave of excitement sweep over her. It was over three months

since Bill had been seconded to St Almas as a senior
relief registrar.

Dear old St Almas, sometimes referred to affection-
ately as the General's mother hospital since so many of
the staff were trained there, as she had been. It would
be lovely to see Bill again. They'd had a nice relationship going, without any hassle. He hadn't written daily
as he'd rashly promised; she'd known that he wouldn't,
but she felt that they would soon pick up the threads
of friendship.

His return couldn't have happened at a better time.
He would put the advent of Tom Hunter in perspective.

CHAPTER FIVE

CLARE was late getting off duty. Miss Cooper, who hadn't been sick for several hours, wanted to tell her how grateful she was to her and Dr Hunter for taking so much trouble over her medication.

'It's dedicated people like you and the doctor who make life in hospital bearable,' she said, squeezing Clare's hand feebly. 'I know I'm going get better now.'

Cathy Kent played up during the evening and was in floods of tears just before Clare was due to go off duty.

'You must get Dr Hunter to look at me—I've got a dreadful pain,' she said to one of the juniors, who, in alarm, rushed to fetch Clare from her office as she was finishing the report.

'I'm afraid he isn't here at the moment,' Clare explained, 'but he left instructions that you were to have some tablets if you were in pain.'

She gave the girl the tablets with some water. Cathy took them sulkily. 'Dr Hunter would come if you called him; I know he would.'

'He can't come running to everyone who wants him. He's got to have some time off duty,' said Clare sharply, and immediately regretted her sharpness. The girl was, after all, going for surgery the next day, and, even if it was run-of-the-mill stuff for the staff, it wasn't surprising that Cathy was nervous. Probably that was making her behave inconsiderately.

'Look, the night staff will fetch a doctor if you still have a pain when they come on duty. Try not to worry, Cathy; you'll be having something to help you to sleep, and this time tomorrow it will be all over.'

The girl refused to be comforted, repeating her demand that Dr Hunter should be sent for. Clare was only too happy to hand her and the rest of the ward over to the night sister.

'They're all yours,' she said cheerfully, dedication going out of the window. 'Good luck to you!'

'Going anywhere exciting?'

'Just to the Castle Arms for a drink with an old friend.'

'Lucky you—enjoy yourself.'

'I will.'

She showered and changed into white jeans and a loose cotton top with bold splashy flowers. Remembering that Bill liked women to wear make-up, she put on a little more lipstick, eye-shadow and liner than usual. She added large hooped earrings, deciding that it was fun for once to over-dress in a casual fashion. Bill, she knew, would appreciate it.

He was waiting for her at a table in the pub garden, a strip of lawn and trees running along the steep sides of the castle walls.

'Sweetie, you look marvellous!' he said, holding her at arm's length, his eyes gleaming with admiration. He bent to kiss her, and as always a hank of thick fair hair fell over his forehead. He brushed it back impatiently with a thin tanned hand.

'You look pretty good yourself. I thought that you might be all pale and languishing, working in town and run off your feet on the wards.'

'The tan comes by courtesy of Sir Ralph and a standing invitation to his swimming-pool whenever I'm free.'

'Well, it certainly looks as if you've had plenty of free time.'

'Rather more as a senior reg than a junior, and it so

happened that a ward was closed for a month, easing the load.'

'Closed?'

'Money and staff shortages—what else?'

It seemed incredible that even St Almas was affected by these things.

They drank cider and ate thick cheese and pickle sandwiches while Bill talked of his work on Sir Ralph's paediatric team.

'He's a great chief,' he said enthusiastically, 'and, Clare, this is what I wanted to tell you that I've not told anyone else. Sir Ralph's offered me a junior consultant's post in his private practice at the end of my stint at St Almas, if I can raise the cash. And he's being very generous about that too.'

She was both flattered and surprised that he'd chosen to give her his exciting news, before, apparently, even his family.

'Does private practice mean no NHS work?' she asked, thinking that it would be a great shame if the health service lost a good doctor to private medicine.

'Lord, no; I wouldn't consider it if it did. I shall almost certainly get a post in hospital at the same time. There's a general shortage of paediatric consultants.'

'And the money to pay for them?' she couldn't help asking rather tartly, recalling what he'd said about a ward being closed.

'Well, there is that,' Bill replied a little sheepishly. 'But Sir Ralph seems to think it will work out OK.'

'He should know, of course,' Clare said firmly, regretting her impulsive, acid remark. It was a shame to spoil Bill's pleasure in anticipating a brilliant future by being over-practical and down to earth. She continued cheerfully, 'Let's drink to the future Mr Bennett, Paediatric Consultant Surgeon.'

They clinked their glasses of cider together, and he

leaned across the table to kiss her. 'What about adding to that,' he said softly, "and the future Mrs Bennett"? You'd be perfect in the role, sweetie.'

Clare was so stunned that she could only stare at him, open-mouthed. She was saved from feverishly trying to think up a suitable reply by a hand decending on her shoulder. She knew before he spoke that it was Tom Hunter's hand. His touch sent a shiver down her spine. He said in a pleased, surprised voice, 'Bill Bennett, by all that's wonderful, fancy seeing you here, and with our lovely deputy matron.' He lifted his hand from Clare's shoulder and extended it across the table.

Bill rose from his chair and shook Tom's hand vigorously. He too looked and sounded pleased.

'Tom, what a turn-up for the books—you, here in a little Home Counties town. Rather different from our last meeting-place!'

Clare, struggling to get over her amazement at Bill's oblique suggestion of marriage, now battled with the surprising knowledge that the two men knew each other. She had yet another small surprise when Jacky Walsh appeared from behind Tom and he introduced her to Bill.

Of course they joined them with their drinks and within minutes the talk was all of Nepal and the Kali Gandak River, on the banks of which the two of them had met several years ago.

Bill, it seemed, had gone out for the WHO for a three-month stint while waiting to take up a hospital appointment in London. He was on a fact-finding mission into deficiencies connected with the dietary conditions of some local tribes.

Tom was in the region with a small group of other professionals on an immunisation programme, part of the worldwide schedule of inoculation against the basic diseases.

But their talk was not so much of medicine, but of the highlight of their stay in that remote and beautiful valley below the great Himalayas. It seemed that a tiger—and there were plenty roaming in that area—had gone berserk and been labelled a man-eater. Tom and Bill had both been involved with the capture of the creature.

Clare, only half listening while her mind grappled with Bill's astonishing proposal earlier, thought that Tom's part in the action confirmed her idea of him as a hunter. She couldn't see him as a run-of-the-mill blood-sports man. Oddly enough, in spite of his lean strength and assertiveness, she didn't think chasing a fox across the undulating English countryside would appeal to him. Nor would shooting inoffensive purpose-bred birds rouse his hunting instincts. The capture of a truly wild and dangerous beast was much more his style.

She had a chance to study both men as they chatted animatedly. Jacky was hanging on to every word and almost sitting in Tom's lap, so closely had she drawn her chair to his. Clare wondered how they had spent the earlier part of the evening, and where and how they might spend the rest of it once they had finished socialising with herself and Bill.

Both men were handsome, each in his own way. Bill with his silver-fair hair, thick and straight, cut short at the back and sides, but left rather long on top. His tan, because of his fairness, was striking, but it could in no way compete with the almost mahogany-brown of Tom's much darker skin.

Tom was wearing a pale blue open-necked shirt and close-fitting matching jeans, a combination that empha-sised his tan and his eyes, and his intense masculinity. The open neck of his shirt revealed a cluster of dark curly hairs on chest and throat. Similar hairs covered

his forearms, visible below his rolled-up shirt-sleeves.
Very sexy, those strong arms and long, lean fingers.

He looked at that moment from Bill, to whom he'd
been giving all his attention, to Clare, and grinned to
find her staring at him. As ever, she felt herself
blushing, and hoped fervently that he hadn't read her
thoughts.

'You're very quiet, Clare,' he said.

'I was listening; it's absolutely fascinating. It must
have been a wonderful experience, living and working
in India.'

'It had its moments,' he said drily, but showed no
more enthusiasm to talk about it than he had on
previous occasions.

Somebody came out from the pub and called time.
The four of them left together, but Tom said immediately they arrived in the car park that he was going to
drive Jacky home. Bill looked disappointed.

'I had hoped that we might go to your place or
Clare's and have a nightcap and continue catching up
on old times.'

'We've other plans, old chap,' replied Tom, throwing
an arm round Jacky's shoulders. She looked pleased.
'The day after tomorrow come to the lodge for supper.
I'll rustle up an omelette.'

'Fine.'

When they had gone Clare suggested that Bill didn't
need to take her back to the hospital in the car.

'It's such a short walk, there's no point in your
having to cross the traffic and then turn round to go
back again.'

She tried to sound casual, but she was so anxious to
be alone to think, and to be rid of him so that she
might do so, that, even to her ears, her voice sounded
strained.

Surprisingly he was very kind and understanding,

and not in the least put out as he might well have been. Although she wanted him gone, Clare found herself resenting a little his easy acceptance of his dismissal. As a man who had just proposed, however casually, he should surely have wanted her company and further discussion on the subject?

But he simply said, mildly but firmly, 'I shall take you back in the car and leave immediately. I remember the rules, sweetie—why do you think that I've asked you to be my wife?'

Of course, he had always understood her atitude to sex and heavy petting. He was one of the men who had rather admired her stand, which was why they had remained such good friends.

There was no point in arguing. She got into his car. 'You didn't even send a postcard while you were away. How do you think I can take you seriously?' she said rather peevishly.

He had the grace to look uncomfortable. 'I didn't realise how much you meant to me until I phoned today. Your voice just triggered off something. Sorry, I can't be more explicit than that.'

His explanation made some kind of sense, she supposed, and gave her even more to think about.

'Did you mean to tell me before your family of the consultancy offer?'

'No, it just seemed so right when we were together.'

'It was a hell of a shock when you said about toasting Mrs Bennett. Are you sure that you meant it, or should I forget all about it?'

'I mean it with all my heart,' he said. 'Even more so after this evening together. We're right to each other. Don't know why I didn't see this before.'

They had arrived at her flat. He kissed her quite chastely on the lips, unfastened her seatbelt, and got out to come round the car and open her door.

'Goodnight, Clare. May I phone you tomorrow during the day, and see you in the evening?'

'Yes, though I'm not sure about the evening. Phone about lunchtime; things are pretty quiet then.'

'Will do.' He bent to kiss her again as she opened the door to her flat, and as usual a hank of hair fell over his face. Impulsively she put up a hand to push it into place. He seemed very young, though he was in his mid-thirties. He seemed vulnerable too, and hopeful, a picture which she took to bed with her.

She had thought that she would lie awake thinking of the momentous event of the evening, but she must have fallen asleep the moment her head touched the pillow. She slept dreamlessly and was awakened by her alarm clock at a quarter to seven.

Clare went on duty, resolving not to be distracted by Bill's proposal of the night before. She would concentrate on work. In any case, in spite of his last words before saying goodnight, she thought it quite possible that this morning he might be regretting his sudden impulse.

Two ward sisters and a staff nurse were still away, so both she and Jacky Walsh had to continue to provide cover. Jacky seemed her usual ebullient self, though she looked heavy-eyed when she arrived at eight o'clock on the ward.

'Fun evening, wasn't it?' she asked Clare, who was doing a general round before taking up her post on Women's Surgical.

'Great fun.'

She had succeeded in putting Bill and his proposal from her mind, but for much of the morning an irritating thought nagged away at the back of Clare's head. What had made the evening so much fun for

Jacky? Surely not just the meeting in the pub, which had been interesting rather than exciting?

She looked tired. Obviously the evening had gone on much later for her and Tom than for herself and Bill, so presumably the 'fun' had started then. Jacky and Tom together, probably—with her friend's somewhat casual approach to sex—for the night didn't bear thinking about. Why it didn't she refused to consider.

Angrily she dismissed these unproductive thoughts and concentrated on Mrs Latham, a patient returned a while before from recovery and now conscious enough to be sat up a little. She had received surgery for the treatment of a femoral hernia. The area of the operation would be sore and painful for quite a while, but it was essential that she should move her legs to prevent a thrombosis, and start breathing exercises to prevent chest complications.

'Mrs Latham. . .' Clare bent over the patient and spoke plainly into her ear '. . .we're going to sit you up a bit now. I've given you some pain-killing liquid through this tube.' She touched the drip where it was inserted in an arm. 'It will lessen the pain, but even if it hurts I want you to try to breathe in deeply and cough gently. Press your hand over the part that has been operated upon.' She took the patient's hand and put it in position. 'Now, breathe away. That's right; well done. Now move your legs.'

She left one of the student nurses with full instructions to special Mrs Latham.

It was at that moment that Tom Hunter came into the ward. He was wearing Theatre greens. His cap was pushed up high on his thick hair, and a mask dangled from his neck. He looked rather rakish. His blue eyes were almost concealed beneath heavy lids.

He stalked down the ward and Clare went to meet him.

'I've come to check the post-ops, Sister.' He looked tired, she thought, and even pale beneath his deep tan. Theatre seemed to have taken it out of him. The heat, perhaps, though he must have endured much greater temperatures in India. Could it be that the illness that had sent him home to England was bothering him? Not that he would ever confide in her, so her question would go unanswered.

Dr Hunter spent time with each patient returned from Theatre. He was especially concerned about Cathy Kent, though in theory her appendicectomy had been straightforward and should present lesser hazards than other abdominal surgery carried out that morning.

'Excusing the pun, I've got a gut feeling about this patient,' he said to Clare as they stood at the end of the sleeping girl's bed. 'I want a close watch kept on her wound. Please report any abnormality to me immediately.'

'Of course. You are expecting problems?'

'I'm not sure, Sister.' He was very formal. 'I can't put my finger on it. Something bothers me.'

Clare was used to surgeons and physicians responding to intangible 'feelings'. She'd had them herself with no firm medical reason to suspect problems. In her book, all the best doctors experienced this 'gut feeling' occasionally. A feeling, as far as she was concerned, that should be respected.

'Would you like a quarter-hourly TPR continued pro tem?'

'Please.'

Clare instructed the junior specialling Mrs Latham in the next bed to perform this duty.

'And look at this patient's wound area each time you do the TPR, Nurse, please. Check for any swelling or change in the region. And, of course, let Staff or me know at once if Miss Kent's temperature or pulse increases.'

'Yes, Sister, immediately.' The sensible student looked pleased to be given such responsibility.

'I'll write up notes in the office if I may,' Tom said quietly, and added, 'Any chance of a coffee?'

'Of course.'

Clare asked the two staff nurses to supervise the lunches and took herself into the office to pour coffee and dispense biscuits for Dr Hunter. She felt that his need at the moment was greater than the patients', all of whom were receiving skilled nursing care.

He gulped down the steaming liquid and held out the empty mug for more.

'Dehydrated,' he said. 'Worked up a real sweat in Theatre. Silly, isn't it, after only a few hours?'

'Not really, if you've not fully recovered from——' Clare hesitated, knowing his reluctance to discuss his illness '—whatever bug you picked up abroad. That's the reason, isn't it?'

'Maybe; it shouldn't bloody well be affecting me now.' He looked angry, frustrated.

He obviously wasn't ready to come to terms with a limiting condition. Perhaps last night's activities with Jacky had something to do with his fragile state this morning. Maybe Jacky's demands had been too much even for this obviously virile man.

In spite of her earlier feelings on the matter, Clare couldn't help a little flutter of amusement at the possibility welling up and making her smile.

'What's so funny, Sister?'

'Nothing.' She pressed her lips together.

He raised his eyelids and his brilliant-blue eyes stared straight into hers. Her heart thumped painfully.

'Nothing,' he repeated flatly. 'Or nothing that you can or wish to tell me?'

Her humour turned to anger, partly with herself for being so easily rattled by him. He was being his usual arrogant self, feeling justified in cross-examining her as if she were a small child.

'It really hasn't anything to do with you, Doctor.' Deliberately she made her voice sound haughty, cold.

'I doubt that.' His certainty that her secret smile was very much concerned with him fuelled her anger. It was as if he could read her mind.

It was an uncomfortable feeling. She asked abruptly, 'Do you want more coffee, or is there anything else I can do for you, Doctor?'

It was his turn to smile, but not a nice smile, she thought.

'Oh, there's a lot you could do for me, Sister, if you were so inclined.'

Clare stared at him, not absolutely sure that he was making an oblique suggestion. A few nights ago he had seemed to understand her attitude towards sex. Now he appeared to be implying that she could change her ideas if it pleased her to, and to please him.

Suddenly he stretched a hand out across the desk and touched one of her hands. The suspect smile had gone.

'Sorry,' he said. 'I'm in a foul mood today. I apologise. Truce?'

It was a generous apology. She couldn't hold anything against him. He was clearly not as fit as he might be, and had been working hard.

She gave him a warm smile. 'Truce,' she said.

'Thank you.'

One of the staff nurses came to the office to ask about a special diet. Clare went off to sort the matter out, and when she returned some time later, Dr Hunter had gone.

The phone rang. It was Bill, ringing as promised to arrange a meeting for the evening.

Clare was shocked to find that she'd not given him a thought. Tom Hunter, even in a bad mood, had succeeded in emptying her mind of Bill and his proposal.

She made the excuse of being busy to be very brief, agreeing to his picking her up at eight o'clock and going somewhere for a meal.

'But nowhere special,' she insisted. 'Just a pub or something like last night.'

'I thought we might be celebrating.'

'Oh, don't be silly, Bill; I haven't had a chance to think of anything since last night. We've got to talk about things some more—surely that's obvious?'

'Of course,' he said, understanding at once, making her feel guilty for being so abrupt. 'You've had a busy morning. Take all the time in the world, sweetie, to think about what I said, but remember that I meant it.'

In spite of its being Theatre day, Clare left the ward at six o'clock. All the patients, including Cathy Kent, were so far making normal progress. There was no reason why she should not go off duty.

'But do ring me, Staff, at the flat if you're not happy about anyone. I'll be there till eight o'clock.'

She wasn't looking forward to going out with Bill, she discovered as she hunted through her wardrobe for another casual outfit. His startling suggestion about marriage seemed slightly ridiculous in spite of his confirmation on the phone that he was serious.

She had known him for some years. They had been very good friends, but nothing more. He had been sorry to leave her when he went off to join Sir Ralph's team. He had, surprisingly, talked about daily letters and frequent phone calls. Perhaps she'd been wrong about his feelings then. Perhaps he'd felt more for her than she realised.

The promise of letters she had dismissed out of hand, but had thought an occasional card or call might have come her way. Even when they didn't come she'd not been bothered. Bill would be frantically busy as a newly appointed senior registrar, striving to impress his superiors and, as a good doctor, devoted to his work.

Having only recently taken up her appointment as deputy matron at the Cottage Hospital when he went away, she was herself wholly occupied with a responsible job. Then, faced with Matron's accident and called upon to take over the running of the hospital, she had needed all her courage and energy to survive the test. Personal plans and pleasure had for several weeks been unthinkable. She was either engrossed with the latest crisis in the hospital or resting and gathering strength to deal with the next.

Only over the last few weeks had she felt able to relax in some small measure, coming to terms with her responsibilities, learning to delegate, taking some time off duty.

She made a face at herself in the mirror. 'I can do without a friend like Bill coming over all amorous,' she told her reflection, and, thinking of Tom Hunter, 'or an arrogant macho doctor throwing his weight about.'

It was a pity that they'd both arrived to shatter her hard-won calm at almost the same time. It was a pity, too, that she couldn't concentrate on Bill's proposal because Dr Hunter persisted in taking up much of her thoughts. She felt guilty at not giving Bill all her attention. Whatever quirk had made him propose he deserved that. Well, at least she would dress to please him again.

'I like it,' Bill said when she opened the door of her flat. 'Give us a twirl.'

The soft folds of the blue and white patterned skirt billowed around her calves, and the white cotton shirt moulded itself to her small high breasts as she did as he had bid.

'Lovely, stunning.'

He pulled her to his chest, pinioned her arms behind her back, and gave her a hard kiss on the mouth.

'Just in case,' he said, 'you should think that I'm kidding or not capable.'

The kiss surprised her and for a moment she was angry, but her anger went in a flash. He had, after all, asked her to marry him. He had respected her wishes the previous evening when he might have resented being sent away, and she had known him for a long time. An honest little voice inside her also reminded her that she had wondered fleetingly if he was 'capable' or sufficiently interested to be passionate.

The evening was a success in so far as they enjoyed each other's company. But, since Bill could not offer more of a reason for his proposal than he'd previously given, Clare still found it hard to accept at face value.

'It seems so odd,' she said, 'that after all these years you should suddenly discover that you are in love with me. To be honest, Bill, I don't think that my feelings have changed towards you. I like you very much; perhaps in time I might grow to love you. I just don't know.'

'Perhaps it was absence that made my heart grow fonder,' he suggested with a grin. 'I'd be willing to risk taking you on, hoping that time would make you change. I'm an optimist, ever hopeful. Will you continue to think about it, Clare?'

She was glad that he hadn't called her 'sweetie' on this occasion. It was an endearment that he used that she found irritating. It seemed to trivialise events, and, whatever else this conversation was about, it wasn't trivia.

'One doesn't dismiss a proposal without some thought. Yes, of course I will think about it. There isn't any rush, though, is there?'

'None at all,' he said airily, 'except that I should like to stake a claim if I'm entitled to one.'

Another small irritation which she squashed. It wasn't as chauvinistic as it sounded, she decided.

He took her back to the flat at half-past eleven, refused a coffee, and drove off immediately.

Clare found that she was both thankful and a little piqued at his readiness to depart, just as she had been the other night.

'There's no pleasing you,' she told herself, getting ready for bed. 'The poor man is wrong whatever he does.'

As she settled in bed it occurred to her that thinking of Bill as 'the poor man', when he had proposed to her, was somewhat unkind.

CHAPTER SIX

THE next day was easier, work-wise. One sister and the staff nurse were back on duty, and the other sister would be back the following day.

Both Clare and Jacky had missed days off, but would now be able to make up their off-duty.

'I'd rather wait till the end of the week,' said Jacky, 'if you want tomorrow off.'

'That'll suit me fine.' Clare thought that she and Bill might be able to have a whole day together as he would still be on holiday. Surely a good idea to gauge how they felt about each other, or at least how she felt about him, since he seemed so sure of his feelings?

In this she was thwarted. Bill rang late morning to say that he'd been summoned back to St Almas.

'There's a heart-lung transplant for a lung-damaged little girl in the offing. As you know, it is often more successful to replace dual organs, even if both are not needed. Her heart's in good condition and is to go to a small boy with valvular problems. Repairs on him have not been successful, so a new heart is his only chance. Sir Ralph wants his usual team on hand for simultaneous surgery.'

'I should jolly well think so,' Clare said, determined not to show her disappointment. 'It's time you left the fleshpots of the Home Counties and returned to work.'

'There speaks the perfect nurse and future consultant's wife,' he said in a smiling voice. He asked her to let Tom know that he wouldn't be turning up for his omelette that evening. 'Why don't you go and share it with him?'

It was exactly what Tom suggested when he called in at the office a few minutes later when she'd passed on Bill's apology for breaking their supper date.

Clare wasn't sure. 'I was going to do several things this evening,' she said. 'I've got a bit behind with my chores this week.'

He looked at her as if he didn't believe her, and she had the grace to blush. She was prevaricating. She knew it, and, what was more, *he* knew it. She wasn't sure of her reasons. One part of her wanted very much to spend the evening with him; the other, inspired mainly by pride, fought against giving in to him without at least showing a token reluctance.

'You don't have to decide this minute.' He was apparently indifferent to her decision. His coolness for some reason made her determined to accept his invitation.

'Oh, I suppose I can leave my odd jobs for another day. The opportunity to savour your culinary talents is too good to pass up.' She hoped she'd hit the right note, sounding as cool and casual as he.

'Good, I make a mean omelette. Shall we say about half-past seven?'

He went off to do his rounds and didn't come back for his usual coffee, but telephoned to say that he had some shopping to do.

'I'm going to give you an omelette to remember,' he said. 'The works,' and then added, 'that is, if you like curry.'

'I love it.'

'Great.'

She found that, as the day progressed, she was looking forward to the evening with Tom and to her day off the following day. Her work load really had been heavy over the past few days, and Bill's arrival and subsequent proposal had added a little more tension. Tonight and tomorrow she would relax. It was just as well that Bill had been called back to St Almas: it would give her breathing space.

Tom and Clare met up again before the evening at Cathy Kent's bedside. Just as the doctor had feared, she had quite suddenly blown up a wound infection. With the sister back on duty there wouldn't normally have been any reason to inform Clare that a patient had medical problems. In this instance, Di Thorpe thought that, as acting matron, she should know that the girl had given false information about her parents and her employers.

Clare felt doubly responsible. In Sister Thorpe's absence she had admitted Cathy to the surgical ward, and taken details of her next of kin. It was galling to find that she had been deliberately misinformed. The present situation with the patient was not acute, but serious enough to warrant advice to the next of kin.

'They don't live in Cornwall, not any more,' said a truculent Cathy. 'They've moved to Wales. I couldn't stand it; I left home.'

'And apparently you left the bank, Cathy; you didn't transfer to here.' She had phoned them on receiving Sister Thorpe's message about the girl. 'The local office don't know anything about you, though they are willing to help if you give me more information.'

Cathy suddenly burst out crying. 'I want my mum,' she sobbed.

'Just you tell me where she is, love,' said Clare, all compassionate for the young girl, 'and I'll get hold of her. I promise she will be here before the night's out.'

Cathy gave her the name of some unpronounceable village in South Wales, and then gave her the phone number.

Clare explained, 'I'm going back to my office, Cathy, to phone from there. You take the medicine that Dr

Hunter has prescribed and do exactly what he tells you. I'll be back with news in a short time.'

Tom caught her up as she was leaving the ward. 'Do you think it was wise to be quite so optimistic?' he asked. 'Supposing her people don't respond as you think they will. You're treading on thin ice.'

'Any mother would respond to a daughter's plea for help,' replied Clare confidently.

'Oh, my dear, I just hope that you're right,' he said, and accompanied her to her office.

Clare was right. Her call to a remote Welsh village elicited an immediate response from loving parents who had been worrying themselves sick over the disappearance of their daughter.

'We'll come straight away, Sister,' said Cathy's loving and tearful mother. 'It will take us about five hours to get to you. Please tell Cathy that we are on our way.'

'With pleasure,' said Clare, putting down the phone and smiling across her desk at Tom. 'It's all right— they're coming,' she told him.

'Who's a clever girl, then?' he said, laughing, and, leaning across the desk, kissed her cheek.

They both went back and told Cathy the good news. In spite of the pain and discomfort caused by the inflammation of her wound and a high temperature, she was a different person. Gone was the sullen mulish expression, replaced by a tremulous smile of pure happiness.

'Rest now, Cathy; it'll be late when your parents get here, but I'll ask Night Sister to let you see them for a few minutes. We'll give them a bed for the night, so you'll be able to see them all day tomorrow.'

The good news concerning Cathy made a good start to the evening and Tom was in an ebullient mood when Clare presented herself at the lodge.

'I've come for my supper,' she said happily, responding to his cheerful greeting.

'And a smashing supper it will be, my lovely,' he replied in a teasing, gentle voice. 'Come. . .' he took her hand '. . .let's go through to the garden; I thought that we'd eat there as it's such a fabulous evening.'

The whole evening had been fabulous, Clare thought, getting ready for bed at midnight. She and Tom had been at ease with each other from the word go. No hang-ups, no uncomfortable moments that she'd half anticipated—the evening had been a harmonious whole.

To start with, they found that they had so much in common, from the drinks—'I've made up some dry martini cocktails,' Tom said, offering her a brimming frosted glass full of pale liquid—to music: George Melly's gravelly voice greeted her on the patio.

'How did you know that I love dry martinis and jazz?' Clare asked with surprise.

'I just guessed. You seemed that sort of girl, and I couldn't imagine you not liking the things that I like.' He gave her one of his brilliant smiles, a smile that lit up his dark blue eyes and accentuated the creases at the corners of his eyes. Her heart responded as usual, but only she was aware of its gyrations. She managed to convey a pleased but cool response to his explanation.

'Yes, I think that I would have put you down as a dry drinks and jazz man too. I suppose that it's not surprising that you discovered it in me.'

Their common interests and the fact that they each recognised them in each other lent an intimacy to the evening.

The omelettes, as he had promised, were delicious—light and fluffy, filled with an exotic curry mixture. For pudding they had a fresh fruit salad with lashings of cream.

'What about a walk round the garden?' Tom suggested, taking her hand.

'I should like that.'

Dr Hunter, Tom's father, was a keen gardener. He had laid out a neat vegetable garden, full of potatoes, peas, beans and carrots and other root vegetables. There was a fruit garden too, with caged raspberries and loganberries and bushes of red, white and black currants. The walls were lined with espaliered peaches and nectarines and cordon apples and pears. It was all utterly delightful and very English.

'The setting suits you absolutely,' Tom said, pausing beneath the huge medlar tree at the centre of the garden, 'with your corn-coloured hair and pale golden tan. I dreamed of women like you when I was in some dusty Indian village, surrounded by dark-skinned, black-haired men and women.'

They were standing close together, facing the lodge, with their backs to the evening sun. The tree cast a giant shadow across the smooth lawn and the herbaceous border, where bees and butterflies still hovered busily.

'Didn't you find the Indian women attractive in their saris and veils? I always think how lovely they look here, but they must look even more so in their own country against the right background.' She was apprehensive for a moment. Even though he'd mentioned India himself, would he react as before when she had tried to talk to him about his travels? It would be so sad if a chance remark marred the harmony of the evening.

She need not have worried, for he answered her without seeming in the least bothered.

'Yes, some of them are quite beautiful, and even those who are not often possess a composure that is very attractive.' He put an arm round her waist. 'But then, so do you, Clare, and you're beautiful too.'

It was natural that he should turn her to face him, and it seemed equally natural that she should tilt back her head to be kissed. His lips found hers, softly at first, and then harder. His tongue probed gently until her lips parted, and with rising passion she responded to his probing.

He pushed her down on to the warm grass and lay beside her, cradling her in his arms. She clung to the lean hard length of his body. He unbuttoned her blouse and slid his hands over her bare breasts, teasing her nipples until they were hard and erect and she moaned with pleasure.

He kissed her naked breasts and she pushed her hands under his shirt and ran her fingers through the thick curly hair.

'Tom,' she murmured. 'Tom, I. . .'

His lips were on hers again, muffling the words that she would have spoken. Then he lifted his head and looked down at her, his blue eyes dark with passion and some other expression that she couldn't read. He eased her gently away from himself and with steady fingers buttoned up her blouse.

'Oh, Tom you can——'

'No, love,' he said firmly. 'That's far enough, I think. Let's cool off, give ourselves a bit of time. I know how you feel about one-night stands. I'm not going to jeopardise our relationship by rushing things. We might both regret it.'

He stood up and pulled her to her feet. 'Come on— coffee and liqueurs before I see you home.'

Astonishingly, the episode hadn't spoilt the rest of the evening. He seemed capable of putting his feelings in place, and she followed suit. True, their eyes met from time to time, or their hands touched, and Clare thought how easy it would be to go back to those tender, tumultuous moments on the grass.

But they listened with pleasure to Ella Fitzgerald while they drank their coffee and chatted without restraint. Tom walked her up the drive to her flat, but even then, when a passionate goodnight kiss might have broken through their defences, he restrained himself. He gave her a gentle kiss on the cheek and she kissed his in return. But his voice when he spoke held a hint of suppressed passion.

'Don't make any mistake about how much I want you,' he said thickly, 'but I repeat what I said the other night, dear girl. We've something special going, but it's fragile; we've both got reasons. . .' He didn't finish the sentence, but stopped and shrugged and turned away abruptly down the path. 'Goodnight, my love, goodnight.'

She lay awake, mulling over what he had said for a long time. What, she wondered, were his reasons for caution? She was pretty sure he hadn't been cautious with Jacky, so why with her? Was he just respecting her wishes about sex? It didn't seem like it, for he'd said quite plainly, 'we've both got reasons'.

She was no nearer solving the mystery when she at last drifted in to sleep. By then her thoughts were all of the loving episode in the garden, and memories of his clever hands about her body filled her dreams.

CHAPTER SEVEN

THE phone rang just before eight o'clock. It was Tom. Clare tried to calm her bounding pulse at the sound of his voice.

'What's wrong?' she asked briskly.

'My goodness, you are pessimistic! What should be wrong?'

'Well, I thought as you were ringing something must have happened in admin or on one of the wards.'

'You think after last night I would only ring on a professional matter?' His voice was soft and gentle. 'You're too work-orientated, and, as a matter of fact, so am I. What about the two of us going off for the day together? We could both do with a break.'

There was nothing more she wanted than to spend the day with him, she decided, but would it be fair to Bill? She told herself not to be ridiculous. Until a few days ago Bill had been just a friend from the past. The fact that he had chosen to propose to her must not prevent her being her own person.

'I'd love to go somewhere away from the hospital.'

'With me?' he asked, and she could hear laughter and something else in his voice.

'With you.'

'You've made my day, love. See you in about an hour, after I've done a round and arranged with one of the local GPs to be on call. Then we can both disappear with an easy conscience.'

It was obviously going to be another hot day. Clare had no idea where they might go. She fished out a rather old but pretty and comfortable strapless sundress in pink and white, and slung a white cotton cardigan round her shoulders. It was odd, she thought, that she didn't have to dress up for Tom, whereas she had given a lot of thought about what she should wear for Bill, even though it was casual clothes.

'I thought we would drive inland,' said Tom when he arrived, looking cool and handsome in white jeans and a white shirt unbuttoned almost to the waist. 'We can follow the river road. I've heard that there is a fabulous pub near Doughton, with super food. It backs on to the river.'

'Yes, I've been there a couple of times,' Clare said as she got into the car.

'You look nice,' he said as he closed the passenger-door.

'Thank you.'

Everything about the morning and their drive through the green and gold countryside was delightful. They stopped for coffee at a pretty thatched tea-house at the edge of a village celebrating its thousandth birthday. There were several other customers sitting on the terrace enjoying their coffee. It both amused and gratified Clare to notice that all the women cast covetous eyes on Tom. He really was incredibly handsome.

She failed to notice the appreciative glances aimed at her, or appreciate what a glamorous image she and Tom projected as a couple, his dark good looks a perfect foil for her fair beauty.

They explored the ancient church with brasses still intact from before the Reformation. There was a list of names on the pulpit of young men who had given their lives in the First and Second World Wars. Tom drew Clare's attention to a tomb on which rested the bronze effigies of Sir Thomas and Lady Clara Bowes-Morton, lying side by side in dignified splendour.

'They might be us,' he whispered, smiling and taking her hand in his. 'The names are almost right, and Thomas's lady is almost as beautiful as you are.'

'Such a fulsome compliment, sir!' Clare swept him a curtsy.

There was the sound of soft clapping, and a rotund little man wearing a cassock, clerical collar and a beaming smile stepped out from the shadows beneath the choir loft.

Tom started to apologise for their levity, but the clergyman waved his apology aside.

'Nothing irreverent about it, sir.' He sketched a small bow towards Clare. 'Your curtsy—very nicely done, my dear. Now did I hear you say that you too are a Thomas and a Clara?'

'My lady is Clare, not Clara,' explained Tom. He was still holding Clare's hand, and he squeezed it gently and looked very pleased with himself. She delighted in his words; they made her feel that she belonged to him. A new experience that she would have rejected as sexist a short while ago, but now found surprisingly enjoyable.

'That's near enough. Now let me introduce myself: I'm the rector of this parish, Donald Reid.' They shook hands. 'Would you like to see our crypt? There are some rather fine tombs down there. More of the family Bowes-Morton. They virtually founded the village a thousand years ago.' He extracted a large key from beneath his cassock. 'Sadly we have to keep everything locked up these days; vandals, you know.'

Clare was on the point of sympathising with him and saying that her father had the same problems with his church. Just in time she remembered that Tom knew nothing of her connection with the rector of her home village.

Half an hour later, driving away from the church and

a waving Mr Reid, Clare decided that she must come
clean about her father. She was almost as bad as Cathy
Kent, concealing the truth about her family connections, and, she reminded herself, with no reason at all
for the deception.

'I have a confession to make,' she announced quietly
in a small voice, wondering how on earth she was going
to explain herself.

Tom took his eyes off the road for a moment and
glanced sideways at her. He gave her what she could
only interpret as a mocking smile, but his voice, when
he spoke, was as usual.

'I thought you might, love; all that. . .' he gestured
behind them '. . .was almost too close to home, was it
not?'

Clare was torn between fury and relief. She was
angry because he had discovered at some point that the
rector of Tottering was her father and had said nothing
to her, relieved because explanations should be easier.

'How long have you known?'

'Oh, since a day or two after we talked about the
Barlows and you were hoping to go home.' He turned
his head and smiled at her again, but this time in a
tender fashion, without mockery. 'I wasn't ferreting.
Jacky mentioned that you were a clergyman's daughter.
Since it was unlikely that there would be two Anglican
priests in one small village, I was pretty certain that the
rector who'd loaned out his tennis court was your
father. We didn't meet. He was away on holiday and
referred to as Gareth or the rector, so the name
Browning didn't ring a bell.'

'I thought perhaps you'd been in touch with the
Barlows.'

'They're on holiday at present.' He frowned.
'Anyway, I don't think I'd have gone out of my way to

trace your home address. It was quite obvious from your manner that you were being cagey about it.'

'I'm sorry; I don't really know why I was so reluctant to tell you about my father.' She watched his strong brown fingers on the wheel and was suddenly overwhelmed by the memory of those same hands on her body. She shivered in the hot sunshine.

'Don't worry about it, Clare. We all have secrets, or create them for protection. Perhaps you wanted to protect yourself from becoming involved with me,' he laughed, 'without, thank God, being successful. For involved we are, don't you agree?'

'Yes,' she replied tremulously, 'I believe we are.'

A great wave of happiness engulfed her at his words. The fact that he was suggesting involvement after so short a time together was not so strange. It was no more difficult to accept than Bill's extraordinary suggestion of marriage after years of mundane friendship.

Tom took a hand from the wheel and placed it over her clenched fingers.

'Relax, love; it's behind us now. Let us enjoy the day and the goodness thereof, as perhaps your father would say.'

Clare laughed. 'You make him sound like an old Bible-thumper, and he isn't, you know—he's very with-it. He'd probably say enjoy yourself and let it all hang out.' And then she added hastily with a giggle, 'Well, within reason.'

'That sounds more like it.'

They smiled at each other and Clare thought that she had never been so happy as in that moment. The sun shone, the birds sang, and she was sitting beside the one man in the world for her.

She almost asked him if he felt the same, but some inherent caution stopped her. It was enough that he'd virtually said that he was in love with her. Don't push it, she warned herself; take it slowly; enjoy what you have here and now.

Lunch was delicious. They ate it on the terrace behind the pub overlooking the garden which ran down to the river. Cold cucumber soup, fresh trout with almonds, and the chef's gâteau of incredible richness. They drank a light German wine with the meal, finishing with freshly ground coffee and Cointreau.

'We'll walk off the wine and liqueur, love, if that's all right with you, and I won't drive for an hour or so.'

Hand in hand, they walked along the deserted path beside the river. The sun was beating down relentlessly. They found a patch of shade beside a clump of tall bushes and sat down on the short, springy turf. Apart from the occasional car driving along the road on the bank high above them, all was quiet. Even the birds seemed to have retired for a siesta, and only a few bees hummed idly in the bushes over their heads.

They sat together, shoulder to shoulder, for a while, placidly watching a family of swans gliding back and forth across the river. They didn't talk much; there seemed no need. A sense of utter peace flowed between them. By mutual consent they eventually lay back on the grass, and Clare wondered if Tom would embrace her as he had last night. But he made no move to do so, seeming content simply to lie beside her, and presently his steady breathing told her that he was asleep.

Carefully she raised herself on an elbow and studied his sleeping face. He looked younger in repose. Most of the tired lines had disappeared, except for those round his eyes radiating out from the corners. Laughter lines, or caused by screwing up his eyes against a tropical sun? she wondered. Black eyebrows, flared into wicked-looking wings at the corners: even in sleep they gave him a sardonic, faintly devilish, expression.

His well-marked mouth, rather wide, looked moistly pink, foiled by his tan, and his aquiline nose more prominent against the flat planes of his cheeks. A hint of a midday beard was evident round his strong jaw.

It was a very masculine face, an aristocratic face, a face which she would love forever.

She wanted to kiss him as he slept, but was afraid of waking him. It was as she was trying to decide whether to risk it that there was a screech of brakes from the road above, and then a tearing sound as though of metal on a hard surface.

Tom opened very blue alert eyes so that she wondered, in the brief moment before tragedy struck, if he had been soundly asleep.

At that moment a car engine whined noisily, and a green estate car seemed to sail past them several feet above the steep bank. It hit the ground at the river's edge, which slowed it down a little as it slid, engine still turning noisily, into the water.

'Come on,' said Tom, pulling her to her feet. 'They'll drown if we don't get them out quickly.'

Even in that horrific moment, as she realised what had happened, Clare was able to admire his calm and immediate response to the situation.

They slid and tumbled down the bank. The riverside was still deserted and the road above quiet. It was uncanny. The car seemed to be floating, with the open windows just above the surface.

Tom slipped off his sandals and jeans—his shirt he had discarded as they came down the bank. He slid into the water, naked except for his boxer shorts. He trod water.

'It's deep,' he said. 'Take care.' He struck out for the car a few yards distant.

Following Tom's example, Clare whipped off her sundress and sandals and entered the water in her bra and briefs. The water was astonishingly cold and made her gasp. It was also, as she got nearer to the car, muddy and full of floating weeds. The car was beginning to sink.

'There are two children in the back,' spluttered Tom, struggling to keep afloat as he reached through an open window. 'We'll have to undo their seatbelts and drag them out through the windows. You try from your side; I'll get the boy from here.'

Treading water, going down beneath the surface every few seconds, Clare managed eventually to get a purchase on the car door and put her hands through the window. She struggled to release the seatbelt securing a little girl who was so shocked that she just stared straight ahead, not crying, just staring.

'It's all right, love, we'll soon have you out,' she crooned soothingly, and at that moment the clasp on the seatbelt sprang open. 'Out you come.' She put her arms round the child and gasped as the car lurched deeper into the water and a rush of water into the back seats almost swept the girl from her arms. But she held on to her and pulled, and the child suddenly seemed to sense what was happening and helped to push herself through the window.

Within seconds Clare had pushed her the few yards to the bank. The child had started crying; the cold water appeared to have broken one shock as it added another.

'Stay there, dear,' she said, and, seeing a bigger child already lying on the bank and guessing that he was her brother, added, 'Stay with your brother.'

'Is Mummy all right?' asked the boy. He looked pale and frightened but wasn't crying.

'I'm going back to help get her out. I'm sure she'll be all right. The gentleman who got you out of the car is a doctor. He'll look after her.'

She swam back to the car, now almost completely submerged. Tom's head bobbed up from beside the driver's door.

'The woman's unconscious, and I can't get at her seatbelt.' He was struggling to hold her head at an angle above water. There was a few inches between the car roof and the water. 'I think the car's settled on something—it's not on the bottom and it's not very safe.'

Clare could see that. The vehicle was rocking gently from side to side. 'What can I do?'

Tom's head bobbed down underwater for a moment, but he kept his hold on the woman's head, using the window-frame to support his arms.

Clare's heart missed a beat. 'Oh, please be careful, please.'

Somehow he managed a grin. 'I'll be OK, love; you go and get help.'

'I'm not going to leave you. . .there must be something I can do here.' She choked on a mouthful of water that splashed up over her face. 'Can't we get her out through the door now that the pressure's equalised?'

'No, Clare,' he said fiercely. 'Don't come any nearer; opening the door might upset the balance. Go back to the pub to get help. It's the best thing you can do.'

She sensed that he was sending her away because he was afraid that she might get hurt, not because it was the best thing she could do. She looked at his face, showing the strain of holding up the woman at an awkward angle, with nothing but a precarious edge of metal to support him. Anything might happen if he had to hang on for much longer. The woman might suddenly regain consciousness and start moving about, throwing the car off balance, taking herself and Tom down to the bottom of the river. The car could tip on him, knock him out.

No way would she leave him, whatever he said; she knew that she would be more help to him on the spot. Even if he was right about not opening the door because of the balance, she could perhaps lean through the other window and help support the driver. Perhaps she could undo her seatbelt and they could ease her out through the driver's window. She looked quite slim.

Breaking through her racing thoughts and the uncanny silence that hung over the river, came the sound of whistling, and round the bend of the tow-path came a boy on a bike. Clare thought that she had never seen or heard anything so welcome in her life.

The boy jerked to a stop as he saw the car in the water, and stared, open-mouthed.

'Go for help!' shouted Tom.

Thankfully the boy responded without question, nodded and said, 'Right!' jumped on his bike, and pedalled madly towards the pub.

Clare moved cautiously through the muddy water to the front passenger side of the car. 'I'm going to try leaning through the window to undo her seatbelt,' she explained.

Tom nodded, knowing that he couldn't stop her now that someone else had gone to fetch help.

'Try not to touch the window-frame, and take several deep breaths and let them out a couple of times before you go beneath the water. There won't be room once you're inside; the level will surge up a bit.'

She hadn't thought of that. She would displace enough water to send it briefly to the roof. Her nerve almost failed at the idea of being in a confined space underwater, but she pulled herself together. She breathed in and out as he had instructed, and wriggled through the window space.

Dirty water whirled about her, making it almost impossible to see. The woman spluttered as water washed over her face in spite of Tom's efforts. She was obviously coming round, both a relief and a hazard.

Clare struggled with cold fingers to release the catch on the safety-belt. Her lungs were bursting. It seemed she had been submerged for a long time, though in reality it was only a few seconds. She felt the catch go and pushed the length of webbing out of the way. Somehow she managed to control her movements so that the water wasn't too disturbed as she backed out through the window and lifted up her head to breathe in fresh air.

'OK,' she mouthed at Tom.

'When you're ready,' he said in what she thought was a much too calm voice. It would almost have been a relief to hear some of the fear that she was experiencing reflected in him. 'Try easing her legs round on to the other seat. We'll make her as horizontal as possible before sliding her out. I'm going to clamp my hand over her nose and mouth before we move her. Her head will have to go under for a moment.'

Clare breathed in and out and bobbed carefully under the water again. She eased herself back through the window and downwards so that she could grasp the driver's ankles. It seemed a lifetime before she was able to get the feet together and then slide her hands upwards to get a grip round the knees and heave up the woman's legs up.

The water slopped around and the vehicle rocked as Tom started to pull the inert body towards him. Clare supported the legs until they disappeared through the window. She backed herself out of the car and shot up for air. It was wonderful to breathe freely again. Across the top of the car she saw Tom on his back, supporting the woman as he paddled the few yards to the bank.

At that moment a group of people rounded the corner of the footpath, led by the boy on the bike.

'Someone's phoned for an ambulance!' he shouted.

He leapt off his bike and helped Tom pull the woman from the river. Somebody else helped Clare clamber up the bank. She was exhausted, but Tom seemed not to notice.

'Let's get her into recovery position,' he instructed.

Together they rolled the woman on to her side and pulled one leg, flexed at the knee, over the other until she was in a semi-prone position. Tom turned her head to one side and opened her mouth to clear it and inspect for dentures, before examining her eyes and taking her pulse.

'Shouldn't she have mouth-to-mouth resuscitation?' asked one of the bystanders.

'She's breathing of her own accord,' said Tom.

'Yeah, but she's bin in the water,' said somebody else.

The woman's son suddenly spoke up. Clare felt guilty at having overlooked him and his sister since she'd come out of the water.

The boy said, 'He's a doctor—this lady said he was— so he knows what to do.'

Clare recovered herself sufficiently to ask if anyone present had cardigans or jackets to wrap round the small boy and girl.

The bike boy said brightly, 'I've gotta towel for swimming—would that be any good?'

'It certainly would. May we have that here for this lady?'

A couple of other people offered jackets and the children, who were shivering more from shock than cold, almost immediately began to look better.

'Here, Doc,' said the bike boy to Tom, 'can I give the kids some Coke? I've got some in my saddle-bag?'

'You certainly can, son—great idea.'

Some blankets arrived, sent along by the landlady of the pub. Very soon after that an ambulance and policemen reached the scene, and they were able to hand over to the officials.

The next hour or so was occupied with making statements to the police, though this was done in the comfort of the pub. The owners were very kind, putting a room with a bathroom attached at their disposal, and lending them clothes while their own, put on over wet, muddy underwear, were taken away and washed and dried.

Everyone was helpful, but Clare began to feel the effects of the afternoon's activities and longed to be on her own with Tom. She caught him looking at her in a rather odd fashion a couple of times and decided that he probably felt the same. But, before they were eventually able to leave the pub and return home, they had to endure another small ordeal.

A reporter from the local paper turned up to interview them about the rescue. Hard on her heels, and much more alarming, came a local television station reporter and cameras.

They had just come from the river where they had taken pictures of the now almost completely submerged car. They would be returning there shortly when the car would be hauled out by crane, and tried to persuade Tom and Clare to be there for photographs while the operation was in progress.

'Local heroes stuff,' said the reporter. 'The viewers will just love it.'

'No, thanks,' Tom said politely but firmly. 'Neither Miss Browning nor I want to be involved; as far as we are concerned, it's all finished and done with.'

The reporter looked disappointed but resigned to his decision. 'I don't think it will go away as easily as that; these sort of accidents tend to get follow-up treatment. But if you're certain about not being interviewed next to the river, you will say a few words in front of the camera here, won't you?'

It would have been churlish to refuse, especially as Mr and Mrs Green, the publicans, had been so kind. They were standing by now, obviously hoping for a little harmless advertisement.

Tom looked across at her. 'Clare,' he asked, 'do you mind?'

She shook her head. 'Not at all.' It would be better to get it over and done with, she thought.

The interview took the form mainly of question and answer, and lasted only about ten minutes, but Clare thought it seemed much longer.

At last they were able to say their goodbyes and leave.

They were both very quiet as they drove back the way they had come earlier in the day. It wasn't just tiredness, it went deeper than that. All the magic had gone. He didn't seem the same man who had called her 'his lady' just that morning. Tom was withdrawn, his profile, Clare thought, forbidding and stern, and she had no reserves left to coax him out of himself. The journey was made in almost complete silence. The accident and their part in it, which should have drawn them closer, seemed to have driven a wedge between them.

They passed a nice-looking hotel at the foot of the Downs. Tom asked if she would like to stop there for a meal. But she recognised it for what it was—a polite invitation—and refused.

It was only eight o'clock when they arrived back at her flat.

'Will you come in for coffee?' she asked, unsure whether she wanted him to accept or refuse.

He refused. 'No, thanks. I think we've had enough of today, don't you? And I'm sure you've had enough of me to last a lifetime.' He gave her a penetrating look from his dark blue eyes, raised his hand in salute, and drove off down the drive.

Now what on earth did he mean by that? she asked herself as she entered her flat.

She was still trying to puzzle it out when she retired to bed and went out like a light from sheer exhaustion.

She slept dreamlessly all night.

CHAPTER EIGHT

THE reporter who had warned them that the interest in the river rescue would not diminish immediately was quite right. The woman and children involved in the accident turned out to be the family of a Scottish MP. When this was known the national Press and television became interested.

Life for Tom and Clare became quite difficult for a week or so. They had to endure more television interviews, talk to newspaper reporters, and, most unnerving of all, speak from a local studio to an interviewer in a Scottish studio in the MP's constituency.

There seemed to be no way out of all the publicity.

'You'll only be followed around by reporters and thought churlish if you don't give in gracefully and get it over with,' said Lady Rachel, chairperson of the hospital trustees board. 'And a little publicity never hurt anyone—it'll be good for voluntary contributions. We'll push the ambulance-equipment appeal harder.'

Clare thought that Tom was magnificently controlled at all the interviews. He was never at a loss for words. He fielded some of the more embarrassing questions about bravery by explaining that, as professionals, they were trained to react in emergencies. But he praised the bike boy handsomely, saying that he wished that everyone would respond as sensibly in an emergency. He suggested that more young people might take up first aid so that they could be ready to help if ever they were caught up in an accident situation.

He quoted the words of the bystander who had

suggested mouth-to-mouth resuscitation. 'He was well-meaning, but it would have been quite wrong to treat the lady that way,' he explained. 'It should only be attempted when someone is not breathing at all, and then with caution and after making sure that there is no obstruction in mouth or throat. It really is a skilled operation.'

'You sound as if you don't approve of this method,' said the reporter.

'No, it's not that, it's a question of the would-be life-giver knowing exactly what to do. I suppose what I'm saying is that there should be more centres available where this and other first-aid skills could be learned.'

'You mean in hospitals and schools, with medical practitioners teaching?'

'Well, it's a thought, isn't it?' said Tom, and then, with one of his devastating smiles, added, 'I've dropped myself and my colleagues nicely into that one, haven't I?'

Lady Rachel, the board, and half the residents of the town thought so too, and were delighted. The Cottage Hospital was bombarded with requests to start teaching sessions.

Tom said, 'I don't mind, while I'm here, spending a few hours a week teaching, but I'll only be around for a short time; it will then be up to my father, who is the permanent medical officer, to carry on.'

His father rang Clare a few hours after the Scottish interview.

'I can't seem to get hold of my son,' he said brusquely. 'When I ring the lodge he's not there—only that damned answering machine—and the hospital switchboard says that he's in Theatre at the moment.'

'He's trying to lie low, I think. The Press and TV won't leave him alone.'

'Do they leave you alone, Clare?' asked Dr Hunter.

'You looked stunning on television.' He sounded rather like his son with his deep sexy voice. Neither of them had a noticeable Scottish accent, but a distinctive burr occasionally broke through.

She felt herself blushing at his compliment and was glad that there was no one in her office to witness the fact.

'I've had some fan letters, Doctor, and so has Tom. It's most peculiar how some people behave when you've been on the box. But he's in the news even more since he spoke about the possible dangers of mouth-to-mouth resuscitation.'

'It had to be said. He was quite right to bring it to public attention. We didn't hear that on the telly up here, but it was reported in the local Press.' He spoke gruffly, as though reluctant to praise his son, but added in gentler tones 'I was glad to see you and Tom out together, Clare. I hope that you enjoyed your outing in spite of its watery finish.'

'We had a lovely day,' Clare assured him, glad that he would never know how it had ended. 'I'll tell him you phoned and get him to ring you back.'

'Thank you, I'd appreciate that.'

After he'd rung off, she remembered that she hadn't even asked how he was getting on. He sounded fine, but was he resting enough, taking his medication and sufficient, but not too much exercise? According to Tom, his sister would see that he toed the line, but, knowing Dr Hunter senior and his stubbornness, she wondered if that lady would be tough enough to control him.

She was glad of the excuse of his father's phone call to get Tom into her office later that day. His father had found him hard to contact, but she found him elusive too. It seemed that only when reporters, hot for news, brought them together did she see anything of him. He otherwise appeared to be avoiding her. He had even stopped having his daily after-rounds coffee with her, sometimes putting his head round the door to say, 'Nothing to report; had coffee on Men's Surgical. See you.'

But he never went out of his way to do so, and pride wouldn't let Clare contact him unless she had to.

There were, of course, professional occasions that neither could, or would avoid.

Mr Sorrell's surgical days came into this category. Since Tom's arrival at the hospital, this consultant seemed to expect his attendance in Clare's office and frequently in Theatre too. Mr Sorrell ignored his registrar's obvious annoyance at this arrangement in his usual high-handed way, often sending him off on quite unnecessary errands. It worried Clare that Tom appeared not to be bothered by this unfair treatment of Cutler, the registrar. She tackled him about it on one occasion.

'It's not fair to Bob Cutler,' she said one afternoon at the end of Theatre and Mr Sorrell's departure. 'He's not the world's greatest surgeon, but he does work hard. Don't you mind that he's being pushed out for you?'

'Nothing's very fair, Clare.' He sounded rather bitter and she wondered if it was for personal rather than professional reasons. 'He's got to be tougher if he's to stand up to Sorrell and consultants of his ilk. Cutler's quite good as a surgeon, but he must push harder. I'm only a temporary aberration. Perhaps seeing his chief's bias towards me will spur him into action.

There seemed nothing more to be said or done. There was a hard streak in Tom that she couldn't break through, and he obviously didn't intend that she should do so. Neither did the conversation lead to Tom's staying in her office longer than was necessary for him to complete his paperwork. Jacky came in to discuss some staff changes. She flirted quite outrageously and openly with him, and he responded in like fashion, agreeing to meet her later for a drink. But he went off as soon as he decently could with a casual goodbye to Clare, remarking that he would see her around.

Today, though, she determined, was going to be different. She had a cast-iron reason for contacting him; his father's phone call.

She left word at the switchboard and on each of the wards, asking him to get in touch with her personally when he was free.

He called in at her office mid-afternoon. If she had harboured any thoughts of making him feel guilty for avoiding her he certainly gave her no chance to reveal it.

He knocked briskly at the door and entered almost before she could invite him in.

'I wanted to see you, Clare,' he said as if she had been the one impossible to get hold of. 'I hope it won't make things difficult, but do you think that we could fix up a time and place for this first-aid teaching session? I think I'm lumbered with it pro tem, even if Dad doesn't want to carry on when he returns.'

She struggled to remain as unmoved by his presence as he apparently was by hers, but it was difficult. For the first time in over a week he was sitting opposite her in what appeared to be a relaxed fashion. His blue eyes regarded her alertly, endorsing the question he had just asked. His manner was cool, businesslike, perfectly polite. We're just colleagues, he seemed to be saying, nothing more. Two senior members of staff discussing a hospital problem. It seemed that he was warning her not to read anything more into his presence there.

She dropped her eyes and said abruptly, 'Your father

rang earlier; he's been trying to reach you. He wants you to ring him back.'

He frowned. 'But I was only talking to him the night before last.' He looked anxious. 'Did he seem all right?'

'We had a perfectly normal conversation. He seemed fine.' She didn't say anything about having the impression that father and son hadn't spoken since the rescue episode. She must be wrong. Presumably Dr Hunter senior just wanted a personal conversation with Tom.

'I'll ring him from the lodge later. Now about this business of first-aid sessions—can you suggest any particular part of the hospital where we might hold it?'

Clare had in fact given it some thought since the interest shown in the project.

'The first-aid unit station seems the obvious choice. We have the equipment there for demonstration purposes, and I'm sure that some of the people who man the unit would be willing to assist. But we need confirmation from the board for permission to use the building.'

'Presumably that means Lady Rachel, yes?'

'Got it in one.' He'd obviously cottoned on to the fact that Lady Rachel was the linchpin of the trustees.

They smiled at each other conspiratorially; for a moment both had their guards down.

He leaned across the desk and took her hands in his. 'Oh, Clare,' he said in a husky, hesitant voice, 'this last week's been hell.'

'I thought you wanted it that way. You've been avoiding me, not I you.' Her hands were trembling, her heart thumping wildly, her eyes locked into his.

'My darling girl.' He brought her fingers to his lips.

The phone on her desk jangled sharply, splintering the soft words that hung between them. Tom swore vehemently, savagely. Clare picked up the receiver with one hand, leaving the other in Tom's grasp.

She listened for a moment. 'Put her hand and arm under the cold-water tap. Dr Hunter and I will be there immediately.'

Tom had let go of her hand and was standing up before she'd finished speaking. 'A burn?' he asked. 'Staff?'

Clare nodded. 'A kitchen assistant; only started work today. Scalded herself with a saucepan of boiling water.'

They were already out of the office and walking fast down the corridor.

A lot of people seemed to be gathered round a small middle-aged woman standing at the sink. They were offering conflicting advice and noisy commiserations.

Clare stood just inside the kitchen door. 'All staff who don't work in the kitchen—out, please, at once.' Three women sidled away but seemed reluctant to leave the scene of the accident. 'Out,' repeated Clare firmly. 'Thanks for your help, ladies, but leave it to Dr Hunter now. We'll keep you in the picture.' She gave them a nice smile. 'Alice, will you get the first-aid box from the cupboard, please?' she asked the assistant cook. Alice bustled away.

Tom said softly as they crossed the kitchen, 'A nice little exercise in management-staff relations.'

He did his own bit in that direction when he examined the scalded arm, complimenting the new kitchen help on her bravery.

'It must be very painful, Mrs Warner,' he said as he gently applied a dry sterile dressing from the first-aid box that Alice eagerly thrust at him. 'You're very brave.' He praised Cook too for her prompt action in putting the injured limb under water, not letting on that he knew that she'd been so instructed.

'Sister told me to do that when I phoned,' said Betty in her straightforward, honest fashion, 'though I thought that's what I ought to do.'

'Well, you did it, and immediately that's what is important—it prevents the skin from getting more damaged. On account of your quick action Mrs Warner will only need simple treatment and her arm should heal nicely.'

He gave them a grin. 'I think perhaps you ladies should come to the first-aid sessions when we start them, don't you? After all, kitchens are one of the most hazardous places to work. Full of lethal weapons like pans of boiling water and sharp knives.'

They all responded to his smile and his suggestion. 'I'm game,' said Cook. 'I did a bit of first aid a long time ago, but after today I realise I don't properly remember much.'

'Well I look forward to your presence, ladies; meanwhile, I think you could all do with a nice sweet cup of tea.' He turned to Clare. 'Will it be possible for someone to take Mrs Warner home presently, Sister?'

'Of course; I'll arrange that. When you've finished your tea, Mrs Warner, please go along to Sister Walsh's office. She's the administration sister and will have to enter this accident in the files. Betty, you'd better go too; Sister will want a statement from you, as head of the department.'

She and Tom left together, but he was almost immediately bleeped with a request to go to Men's Surgical.

'Have you got hold of the new house surgeon?' he asked, and apparently received confirmation of this. 'I'll be with you shortly. Meanwhile ask Dr Wyatt to carry on; he knows what to do.'

They stopped for a moment in the corridor after he'd used the phone. He leaned back against the wall, white coat thrust half behind him as he jangled change in his trouser pockets.

Clare wondered if he knew how devastatingly virile and masculine he looked. Probably, though without conceit, she decided, he would accept it as a fact of life.

'I'd like to pursue our conversation from where we were interrupted,' he said in a low gravelly voice. His eyes, a minute before just friendly as he'd spoken to the kitchen staff, were now dark and blazing with passion.

Two young nurses passed by, mumbling a greeting to both doctor and deputy matron, but their admiring eyes were on the handsome medical officer. Clare heard them giggling as they moved down the corridor. She wondered if they could sense the strong tide of feeling that was flowing between her and Tom, or whether they were fantasising about him with girlish self-consciousness. She rather thought, and certainly hoped, the latter.

She could feel the heat from his body as they stood close together, and it wasn't just because it was a hot afternoon. Suddenly it seemed not to matter if he demanded everything from her. She was ready and willing to give in to this rising tide of passion that was swamping her, and, if the look on his face was anything to go by, overwhelming him. She wouldn't let him draw away from her any more as a gesture towards her reservations over sex. Neither would she let him freeze her out as he had done after their riverside experience.

She would convince him that he might make love to her and it wouldn't spoil their relationship even if he didn't want commitment.

It was odd to have all these personal intimate thoughts swirling round in her head in the middle of the clinical hospital corridor, with staff passing to and fro at frequent intervals. She felt as if she was playing truant from her cool professional self and was almost an open book for anyone to read and interpret. The idea lent a piquancy to the situation.

His bleeper went again and he picked up the nearby wall phone. 'Yes, all right, Sister, I'll be with you after I've been to Men's Surgical.' He turned back to Clare. 'I must go. The hell of it is that I can't see you tonight— I've an engagement that I can't break. Look, I'll phone you before I go out; we'll fix something for tomorrow.' He turned away, saw that the corridor was empty and turned swiftly back. 'Goodbye, my darling.' He kissed her hard and then went away with long strides.

His kiss was almost her undoing. Slowly, she returned to her office, trying to quell a pounding heart and subdue the bright love-light that she knew shone in her face and eyes. She must present a calm face to the world and concentrate on work for another hour or so. It was a bitter disappointment that Tom wasn't able to see her tonight, but she told herself that this was just as well. Let them both get used to the new—or rather the now acknowledged—situation that existed between them before being alone together again.

There was a host of things that she had to see to: several telephone calls to make, and a meeting with the ward sisters to sort out staffing levels over the next few weeks, always a problem in the summer months, however well planned ahead of time. She was glad to be busy—it kept her mind off Tom and the delights of a future, however limited in time, with him as her lover.

For now she had no doubts about that at all. She would convince him, if he still needed convincing, that it was the natural thing for them to become lovers.

She wrenched her mind back to the present and Sister Thorpe, who was suggesting a pool of part-time nurses—old staff who might be prepared to come back for a few hours a week.

'Could we get in touch with them?' she asked.

'Why not?' replied Clare. 'Could you do that, Jacky; a personal phone call or letter?'

'They all know we need them; we always make it clear when they leave that they only have to get in touch.' Jacky sounded rather disgruntled, unlike her usual cheerful self.

'But a direct approach, asking for immediate response, might produce some results. It's rather different to considering a future proposition. Will you give it a try?' Clare wondered at Jacky's depression. It was so uncharacteristic. Perhaps she found it more noticeable because of her own euphoria.

The long afternoon, with its dizzy heights of emotion between herself and Tom and the more mundane chores of office, eventually came to an end. Clare made her way up the drive to her flat in excited anticipation of his phone call, longing to hear his deep, velvet-soft voice. The voice that this afternoon had been gravelly with pent-up feeling. She told herself not to be ridiculous; it was only an hour or so since he'd been talking to her, an hour or so since he'd kissed her hard on the mouth in the busy confines of the hospital corridor.

Telling herself to be sensible made not a scrap of difference: she still looked forward to his call with mounting excitement.

The phone was ringing as she entered the flat. She rushed to pick up the receiver with a trembling hand. She was quite shocked and astonishingly disappointed when Bill's voice, and not Tom's, spoke in her ear.

'Hello, sweetie,' he said brightly. 'I've got a free evening at last, but not enough time to get all the way down to you. What say we meet halfway. . .say the Friary Inn at Hindhead—are you game?'

She was stunned into silence for a moment. For, although she'd had qualms about getting closer to Tom since Bill had proposed, the afternoon's events had wiped all her doubts and Bill from her mind. She was almost ashamed to acknowledge even to herself how easily she had cast him aside. It was true that she didn't owe him anything in terms of promises made or received, but to forget him so readily seemed rather shabby.

Of course she'd been totally honest with him about his proposal, putting it into perspective as she saw it. Refusing to be pushed into a decision, stating her feelings fairly and squarely. Now she must seize the opportunity of an evening out with him to set the record straight. Unreservedly she must refuse him, however much he might try to persude her otherwise and however fleeting might be her affair with Tom.

Rather breathlessly she said that yes she would meet him.

'Oh, great. Put on your glad rags, dress up a bit tonight, darling. The Friary is a rather dressy place, you never know who you're going to bump into there.'

'Yes, I know, I've been there a few times. Can't we go somewhere less obvious?'

'Table's booked,' he said sharply, adding in a more conciliatory tone, 'Don't make waves, old thing; anyone would think that you were ashamed to be seen out with me.'

'What, with a handsome beast like you?' she replied in a bantering fashion, immediately regretting her reluctance and determined to get the evening off to a good start.

'That's my girl.' He was quite reassured by her reply.

* * *

She took the phone into the bathroom with her as she showered, in readiness for Tom's call. He'd still not rung by the time she'd put on a floaty blue and white dress caught at the waist by a narrow silver belt, emphasising her slenderness. Flowing filmy sleeves were held at the wrists by silver bands to match the belt. She fastened on long drop earrings and slipped on blue velvet sandals. Bluey-green eye-shadow made her grey eyes glow, and coral lipstick accentuated her nicely shaped mouth. She brushed her short fair hair till it gleamed, and felt ready for the fray, though she wished that it were Tom and not Bill with whom she would spend the evening.

She was ready, and Tom still had not rung. If she didn't leave soon she would be late at the restaurant.

The phone sprang into life. 'Clare, sorry I'm late, got held up on Surgical.'

'Problems?'

'Dealt with and left in the capable hands of my young colleague. Don't you start worrying, for heaven's sake, my darling. Just sit at home and think of me having to endure a dull duty evening with an old buddy of Dad's.' His voice dropped to a soft whisper. 'Dearest girl, I wish with all my heart that I could be with you tonight.'

'Me too,' she said warmly.

He gave a throaty laugh. 'We'll make up for it tomorrow, I promise. Now, tell me when you can be free and I'll move mountains to make sure that I'm free too.'

'Not till the evening, I'm afraid, but I will get off sharp.'

'I'll collect you at six, not a moment later.'

'On the dot.'

Much later, driving to Hindhead, she remembered that she hadn't told him that she was going out. Never mind, she would tell him tomorrow and why it was

important for her to see Bill. Meanwhile she would
savour his words and hug to herself the thought that
tomorrow night would be a new beginning for them
both.

CHAPTER NINE

CLARE arrived at the Friary Inn a few minutes after the time she had agreed to meet Bill. He was waiting in the car park.

'Sweetie, you look great,' he said enthusiastically as he helped her from her car. He pulled her into his arms and gave her a hug and a kiss. She was happy that he didn't seem too sentimental or romantic, just robustly friendly as he had been in the past. But a moment later she realised why he was restrained. He had something on his mind; he felt guilty. A wave of relief passed over her. He was probably regretting his proposal and she could refuse him without hurting him or his pride.

His next words dashed her hopes of an opportunity to talk quietly with him, and also explained his guilty air. 'I've a surprise for you, Clare; I'm sorry, but I really couldn't do anything about it. Sir Ralph and Lady Fox are here. It was Sir Ralph in fact who booked the table. They are hosting us.' His next words sounded ominous. A cold feeling of foreboding overwhelmed her, though she wasn't sure why. 'I couldn't really get out of it.' A hank of hair dropped down over his forehead as he bent over to explain apologetically.

'You could simply have said no.'

'To my chief!'

'He doesn't own you.'

Bill looked sullen. 'You know how it is in our profession. You're a nurse; you understood when I had to whiz back to St Almas for those transplants.'

'That was quite different—that was work, that was being a good doctor. For heaven's sake, there's no comparison with that and giving up your free time at the whim of Sir Ralph, however good a chief he might be.'

She couldn't contain her anger. To think that she had grabbed the chance of seeing Bill in order to break it gently that she couldn't marry him, and was now faced, instead, with having to be nice to his boss for the evening.

'Oh, hell,' he said dejectedly. 'I'd no idea you'd react like this, and the old man's in great form and dying to meet you. You will be decent to him, won't you?'

Clare stared at him in amazement. 'What on earth do you think I'm going to do—stalk in and tell him off in front of a room full of people? What do you take me for, Bill? I know how to behave. It's just that I particularly hoped that we'd have the evening alone together to talk.'

He was looking so distraught that she began to feel sorry for him. He cheered up at her words. She hoped that he hadn't misunderstood her.

'I'd much rather be alone with you too, sweetie, but this evening's important to me. I think Sir Ralph's going to confirm my appointment as his junior. He's old-fashioned about these things, likes to do them with a flourish.'

'Then we'd better not keep the old boy waiting,' she said, giving in gracefully with a nice smile.

'That's my lovely girl.' He kissed her quickly, lightly on the cheek.

They walked into the restaurant arm in arm.

Sir Ralph and Lady Fox were delightful, and by the warmth of their welcome and subsequent conversation almost made up for Clare's earlier disappointment. She remembered Sir Ralph from her student days when he'd delivered some stimulating lectures on paediatric nursing. Lady Fox had at one time been a nurse and, in spite of their age-gap and modern nursing techniques, they found much in common to discuss.

They were about halfway through their delicious meal when Sir Ralph dropped his bombshell. He motioned to the waiter to fill up their glasses with the champagne that was standing at the side of the table and stood up.

In his booming voice, which Clare remembered from his lectures, he announced, 'We have two important events to celebrate tonight; one, my young colleague's elevation to a consultancy in the practice——' he bowed towards Bill '—and two, the forthcoming engagement of Bill to the lovely Clare.'

Lady Fox stood up with her husband and raised her glass. Bill went a fiery red and gave Clare an apprehensive look. Clare felt her cheeks going pale.

Sir Ralph and Lady Fox sat down and looked expectantly at Bill.

It was Clare who recovered first. She tapped Bill playfully on the hand. 'Say thank you, darling,' she said, trying to sound loving and a little shy, quelling her anger which, for their hosts' sake, she must not give way to.

Bill rose to his feet, gave her a grateful smile and began a little speech of thanks to Sir Ralph and Lady Fox.

While he was speaking, Clare tried to make sense of her chaotic thoughts. One thing was crystal clear. Bill had led the Foxes to believe that she had agreed to marry him. Of course, Sir Ralph, being an old-fashioned-type medic, would prefer his practice colleagues to be married. Being able to produce a fiancée must have clinched the job. Bill hadn't just proposed because he suddenly found that he was in love with her, but because he realised that a wife was necessary for promotion.

To do him justice, he probably hadn't reasoned it out coldly and clinically, but responded to some subconscious promptings. He had talked himself into believing that he was in love with her, and their close friendship had enabled him to slip easily into the role of lover.

For a minuscule moment she wondered what it would be like to be married to Bill. To be wrapped around with a cosy sort of love and financial security. To be involved in his world of paediatric medicine, with a professional understanding of his needs. To be a wife and companion to such a man could not be all bad. Briefly, she allowed herself to contemplate a possible alternative to the unknown encounter with Tom. A future with him would always be uncertain.

Bill finished his speech. They all drank more champagne. Clare made herself eat the rest of her dinner, conscious that she had to drive back and had drunk more than she normally would. The delicious food tasted like sawdust.

At last the ghastly evening came to an end and she and Bill stood side by side seeing the Foxes off in their Rolls-Royce.

Sir Ralph, heavily gallant, had patted Bill on the back and kissed Clare's hand. 'We should be seeing you off, as our guests,' he said in an avuncular manner, 'but I dare say you young people want a moment to yourselves.'

It was the last thing that she wanted. Bill had evidently taken her acceptance of the toast to their engagement as her willingness to marry him. She had realised this as he'd made his thank you speech and from his behaviour towards her as the evening had worn on. His momentary embarrassment at Sir Ralph's announcement had given way to elation, which she had been able to do nothing about without giving him away.

As soon as the car was out of sight she shrugged off his arm and said in a quiet, cold voice, 'I'm going now, Bill. I don't ever want to see you again. I've done my bit this evening; it's up to you how you explain our non-engagement to your chief.'

He was so surprised by her action that she was halfway to her car before he caught up with her.

'I don't understand,' he said plaintively. 'You seemed to be pleased. I know it was a shock, the old boy coming out with the bit about our engagement before you'd formally agreed, but surely there's no harm done? He only anticipated things by a few hours.'

'You're so crass, you're incredible! What the hell makes you think that I was going to say yes? Before this evening I wasn't sure of your motives; now I know what they were.'

'I don't understand,' Bill repeated. 'I love you!'

'Like hell you do! For a clever and good surgeon you're amazingly ignorant when it comes to personal relationships. Do you really believe that you love me? Can't you see that it was convenient for you to have a wife?' By now she was feeling more sorry for him than angry. But she was exhausted and wanted only to get away. 'You'll just have to sort it out for yourself, Bill. I hope that you still get your consultancy; you deserve that.'

She got into her car and drove away fast, leaving him standing, looking quite helpless and very handsome in his dinner jacket and black tie.

'You'll have no difficulty replacing me with a docile wife,' she muttered cynically to herself as she turned on to the busy road back to the Cottage Hospital.

* * *

Clare didn't sleep very well, constantly waking and going over the events of the evening. At times she blamed herself for even giving Bill the slightest encouragement about their relationship. Then, more practically, she was able to convince herself that it was he, and not she, who had pre-empted the situation. The trouble was that in spite of what had happened she still liked Bill. She was certain that he hadn't deliberately set out to deceive himself or her when he'd said that he loved her. After all, the dividing line between love and warm friendship was slight, surely?

In her heart she was weighing the feelings she had for Bill against the overwhelming and ecstatic sensations inspired by Tom. Was the one more like the real thing—love—than the other? Did it mean that because the sound of Tom's voice or his touch made her bones turn to water he was the only man in the world for her?

She had thought so only the day before; she had been certain that, however brief their lovemaking might be, Tom was her one and only man. Now, in the light of day, reviewing her emotions when Sir Ralph in all innocence had congratulated them on their engagement, she admitted that she had experienced for a moment an odd feeling of tranquillity, of belonging, of security.

Seeing the Foxes, immutably fixed in their affection for each other, contemplating a future secure in every way, Clare found herself considering the possibilities of a gentle marriage. A marriage based on friendship, not on high romance, fluttering heartbeats, an erratic pulse or the constant aching awareness of the person one loved.

Surely, as a mature woman, she should be able to consider such a proposition?

She despised herself for such thoughts, but couldn't quite shake them off.

Tom wanted her physically, as she wanted him. But he had hang-ups about a long-term relationship, although she had no idea why. He must have had affairs, serious ones, probably, since he was in his late thirties. Had they influenced his reactions towards other women? Towards herself? Although he accepted and even commended her attitude to one-night stands, did he want to, or would he find it easy to take up even a brief relationship? Yesterday he had made it clear that he desperately wanted her whatever the consequences. But then yesterday he had been in an ebullient mood. Would he feel the same today?

In the few weeks that they had known each other they had hit both highs and lows. If it was offered to her, could she live this kind of life?

Her future, and the man that she might spend it with, seemed fraught with problems. The glow that had set her on fire yesterday when he had kissed her had faded. The events of the evening with Bill and the Foxes, followed by a bad night, had left her feeling irritable and unsure of herself and her emotions.

Work was the only constant factor in her life that gave her solid pleasure and satisfaction. Or was it? Even on this golden summer's morning the anticipation of a day of responsibility and decison-making failed to ignite her enthusiasm.

She walked down the drive to the hospital with head high and long jaunty steps. No one, she vowed, would sense her inner turmoil or see her depression, least of all Tom Hunter.

CHAPTER TEN

TOM HUNTER was in fact the first person Clare saw as she entered the hospital at the end of the long main corridor. He was coming towards her, striding along, white coat flying, his head bent to hear what his colleague was saying. He and his companion made to turn off into a side-ward, but Tom raised his head and saw her. He lifted his hand in salute, and even at that distance she could sense that he was pleased to see her.

She replied to his greeting with a wave, hoping that he wouldn't read into it any of her unsettling thoughts as he approached.

'Hello. . .' he hesitated and she guessed that he had been about to say 'darling' but changed it to '. . . Sister,' when a nurse passed by.

'Good morning, Doctor.' She was glad that circumstances made it easy to be formal. 'Did you enjoy your evening with your father's old friend?'

He moved close to her; his eyes were very dark. 'Hated every minute of it; not my host's fault, it was yours. Couldn't get you out of my mind. The old boy was quite mystified by my lack of response at times. I could see him thinking, What's wrong with old Hunter's lad? Must be all those years in foreign parts.' He grinned and looked quite boyish.

Clare glanced nervously up and down the corridor. For a moment it was empty and she was afraid that he might repeat yesterday's kiss. With her mind in such tumult she had no wish for a close encounter of any kind. Her attitude must have betrayed her feelings.

121

He frowned and moved slightly away from her. 'What's wrong?' he asked sharply.

'Nothing——' she shook her head '—it's just that I have a lot on this morning, I. . .' She didn't know how to finish.

Several people came through the front door and noisily down the corridor towards them. Most of them called a good morning to which she and Tom replied. The receptionist arrived in the hall just behind them.

Tom said softly, 'You don't seem very pleased to see me. What's happened?'

'Nothing,' she lied. 'I've just go to get on, that's all.' His nearness was producing all the usual signs and symptoms of pounding heartbeats and a bounding pulse. A moment longer with him and she would be back where she was yesterday afternoon, responding to his every whim, forgetting his moodiness, his power to dictate the way their relationship should go.

She must have time to think, to be in control of herself before entering into a discussion with him. Besides, the present time and place were quite unsuitable for intimate dialogue, with staff coming and going. She needed to get away from him.

'I must go,' she said breathlessly, trying not to respond to his overwhelming masculinity as he looked down at her, eyes boring into hers. 'Tom. . .' her voice was shaky '. . .please, I must go; see you this evening.'

'I'm not stopping you,' he said, taking a step backwards to indicate that she had plenty of room to move. 'Till this evening, then.'

His voice sounded harsh, unforgiving, but perhaps that was her imagination. She slipped past him and made for her office, aware of his eyes on her back as she walked away from him.

At that moment the front double doors were thrust open and Trevor Reynolds, an orderly, staggered into the corridor. One trouser leg was dark and wet with blood, which continued to pour down in a sticky torrent as he hobbled in.

Tom was with him in a few quick strides. Clare threw open the nearest door, which happened to be the telephonist's office. The two women at the switchboard gaped in surprise as Tom, almost carrying Trevor, appeared in the doorway.

Clare pushed chairs and a small table aside.

'Down here,' she said, and helped Tom lower the man to the floor.

'Feel faint,' he mumbled, before passing out.

Tom kept a hand clamped over the gash in the man's leg, but spurts of blood were oozing between his fingers through the material of his trousers.

'First-aid box, please,' Clare said sharply to the still gaping telephonists, 'and one of you phone for a porter and a stretcher, and then Men's Surgical. Tell Charge Nurse what's happened and ask him to get a side-ward ready.'

The two women sprang into action. Tom raised the injured man's leg as high as he was able. Clare whipped out her scissors and began cutting the trouser leg above the wound.

'Now?' she asked when she had finished.

Tom nodded and eased his hand up just enough to allow her to pull the drenched bottom half of the trouser leg down and off. Even that slight easing of direct pressure on the wound caused a further gush of blood.

Tom looked grim. 'He'll be in failure if we don't stop this soon. For God's sake, give me a pressure-pad.'

Clare was already searching in the first-aid box, unfortunately a fairly basic one with mostly small dressings and bandages. She discovered a triangular bandage, stripped the protective coverings off several

small bandages, wrapped them in the triangular bandage, and, at another nod from Tom, pressed the thick
pad over the wound as he eased his hand away. She
secured the pad with a length of tape.

Tom pulled over a chair and supported the injured
limb on it, so that he was free to loosen Trevor's
trousers and shirt collar and make sure nothing else
was restricting the flow of blood back to the heart.

Trevor opened his eyes and looked blearily at them.

'It's all right, old chap,' said Tom. 'You've busted a
vein in your leg; afraid you're bleeding like a stuck pig,
but we've got it in hand.'

Clare was taking Trevor's pulse. 'Improving,' she
said softly to Tom. 'Better volume.'

Trevor shivered and Clare took off her cardigan and
draped it over his chest. One of the telephonists offered
her jacket and Trevor managed a wavering grin.

'I'm getting the full treatment, Doc, aren't I?' he
said to Tom.

'Some blokes have all the luck,' Tom replied, giving
the man a smile.

Blood began to ooze through the pressure-pad in
spite of the limb's being elevated. At that moment the
porter appeared with the stretcher. Clare snatched off
the protective draw-sheet and with Tom's help fixed
that too around the patient's leg.

'Hello, mate,' said the porter, 'what you bin at,
then?'

'Busted a vein, apparently; bashed it against the car
door——'

Tom interrupted. 'Well, let's get this show on the
road; the sooner I can get you to the ward and stitch
you up, the better.'

He and the porter lifted Trevor carefully on to the
stretcher, and Clare exchanged the jacket and cardigan
for a blanket.

'Thanks, Sister. Will you come and see me when I'm warded?'

'Nothing in the world would stop me, Trevor,' she replied, smiling.

'Almost worth getting bashed up for,' said the porter to Trevor.

'Not 'alf,' replied Trevor.

Tom caught her eye as he took up his place beside the trolley, keeping the damaged leg elevated.

'My sentiments exactly,' he murmured softly so that only she could hear.

She felt herself blushing as she turned away to thank the telephonists for their help.

The whole episode had taken about half an hour. Clare hurried to her office, aware that she would have to work hard to make up for lost time. She and Tom had as always worked together in perfect harmony. What a pity that they couldn't emulate this professional smoothness in their personal life.

From the moment Clare arrived in her office she was frantically busy. Work took her over, and whatever reservations she'd had about its being a panacea to all things dispersed as the morning wore on. In fact she hadn't time to think about personal matters. She was happily absorbed as always in finding solutions and settling problems to the exclusion of the unwelcome thoughts that had plagued her at the start of the day.

Generally she did her round in the morning, but today there would only be time to visit some of the wards before lunchtime. She would leave Maternity and Long-Term Medical till the afternoon. Being busy was reason enough to have something sent up for lunch in her office rather than going to the staff dining-room. A choice she made unconsciously, but which she later realised was a neat way of avoiding Tom should he be there.

Hard work had obliterated her doubts during the morning, but the quiet few minutes that she gave herself to eat a chicken sandwich allowed her thoughts full rein again. Resolutely she pushed them out of her mind as she tidied herself up ready for the rest of her round.

She stayed only a short time in the long-stay unit. Many of the elderly patients had visitors on this lovely summer afternoon, and were being wheeled or helped around the garden. She said hello to these in passing, and concentrated on the few without visitors who were sitting out on the veranda enjoying the sunshine.

Mrs Fry was busy with her crochet work, somehow doing exquisite stitches in spite of her arthritic hands.

'For my great-great-grandchild, Sister, due any minute now.'

'You must have married very young, Mrs Fry, to have a great-great-grandchild.'

'I was seventeen and my husband nineteen, and we were happy together up to the day he died, and that was only two years ago.' Tears gathered in her faded blue eyes. 'I still miss him as if it were yesterday.'

Clare said a little awkwardly, rather surprised at the strength of feeling the old lady exhibited. 'It must be a comfort, having a big family around you.'

'It's what it's all about, Sister, isn't it? Family. One of the great-grandchildren will be in to see me on the way home from school or college. One of them comes in every day. And this evening one of my boys will be in. We're a close family,' she added unnecessarily.

Clare reckoned that 'one of her boys' must be sixty-five at least. She spoke to the other patients on the veranda. One of them was Ruby Dowd, a spinster lady of nearly a hundred, who'd listened with interest to

what Mrs Fry had to say. They were both strong-
minded old ladies who had a sort of gentle running
feud going. Each of them took every opportunity to
attempt one-upmanship on the other.

'I haven't got any family, Sister,' she said in her
surprisingly firm voice. 'But then, I never have had,
not blood family, that is; the families I've worked for
have always been my family.' She looked round trium-
phantly, with a special look at Mrs Fry. 'I had postcards
from three of them this morning. Look. Of course,
they all have important jobs and most of them work
abroad, so they can't come too often. But they all keep
in touch.'

It was perfectly true, Clare knew. Nanny Dowd
probably had the biggest constant postbag in the hospital, and, when her correspondents did come to see
her, they came in droves. Usually in Rolls-Royces and
Jaguars, and several generations together. All calling
her Nanny, all bringing expensive gifts and obviously
lots of love.

Two elderly women, she reflected, each having led
full but totally different lives, but each of them doting
on family of one sort or another. Like her own family,
with her loving parents providing a safe, secure background for herself and her three brothers.

Ironically it seemed that this afternoon's experience
in the long-stay unit mirrored the feelings she'd had
about the Foxes last night. It was as if she was fated to
come into contact with reminders of marriage and
stable relationships, at a time when she was confused
about her own future.

She had been so certain yesterday about how she
would respond to Tom's kind of loving, however brief.
She'd been prepared to—no, *wanted* to throw over
years of restraint that both unbringing and inclination
had so far dictated. It hadn't seemed to matter then.

Nothing mattered except the fulfilment that only Tom could give her by making passionate love to her. The memory of the evening at the lodge and his hands teasing her body into awareness made her shiver in the hot sunshine that flooded the corridor as she made her way to Maternity.

In Maternity there was much excitement. A baby boy had been born only a short while before. No matter that this was a recurring event in the unit: a new baby still brought a touch of magic to the day.

'Renews my faith in human nature,' Clare could almost hear Dr Hunter senior say.

At that moment Dr Hunter junior came out of the delivery-room. He and Clare met in the short corridor between Delivery and the main ward. He looked, as always, devastatingly handsome in Theatre greens.

'We seem fated to meet in corridors, Sister,' he said formally, making her a little bow. His eyes had sparked into life as he had come face to face with Clare, and now glowed in the special way that he seemed to reserve for her.

'I was thinking about your father,' she blurted out, to cover the confusion that automatically possessed her at the nearness of him. 'He loves Maternity.'

'Yes, I know. I'm beginning to understand why.' His voice was soft and incredibly gentle as he looked straight into her eyes.

She felt herself blushing. His words immediately conjured up a Tom Hunter different to the image of the man who had been plaguing her since last night. At this moment he could slot into the role of family man without effort. Maybe there was more of his father in him than he was aware of. Lurking beneath the occasional austere façade, or the dashing character who flirted with Jacky, or the passionate but restless man she had glimpsed, was perhaps a man ready to settle down to domesticity.

The idea hit her so suddenly that it took her breath away. In all the scenarios she had imagined with Tom as the main character he had never figured as a run-of-the-mill husband and father. In her mind she had settled for a hopefully long romantic relationship, and had been quite prepared for a short, possibly painful liaison if that was all that was on offer. The reason why Bill's proposal had made such an impact was that it represented the opposite of what she might expect from Tom.

She looked at this dark, tall, gently smiling man, and smiled in return.

'Oh, Tom, I'm so pleased to hear you say that.'

'Am I back in your good books?'

She laughed a little self-consciously. 'I don't know what you mean; did I ever say that you were out of them?' After all, he couldn't know the way her mind had been working half the night and this morning. He was only guessing about being out of favour.

It sounded arch as she said it. It was the sort of remark that Jacky might make, and it would sound natural and amusing coming from her. Clare felt awkward, but couldn't think of anything else to say that would fit the occasion. She didn't want to be heavy and solemn. She wanted to keep the situation light. She wanted to leave it to Tom to explain everything. He must unravel her muddled thoughts and make sense of them.

A great wave of happiness and relief engulfed her. Tom would be in charge. He would make everything come right. How could she ever have doubted that they belonged together? She beamed at him and he grinned back in return as if he had divined her thoughts.

'We'll have a wonderful evening,' he said huskily. 'And it'll be much less public than this, I promise.'

One of the maternity nurses emerged from the delivery-room.

'Come to see our new arrival, Sister?' she asked.

'Please, if I may. I won't be in the way?'

'Not now, it's celebration time,' the nurse replied cheerfully.

Tom shepherded her through the door. Clare was very conscious of his hand beneath her elbow and hoped that it would pass unnoticed by the staff. She need not have worried. The centre of attraction was the baby and the young new parents. All three were just about to be moved into the side-ward.

'Sister,' said the new mother, looking remarkably relaxed as well as happy, 'look at my son.'

Clare bent to study the baby already looking clean and fresh, though still very red and wrinkled from his efforts to enter the world.

'He's beautiful,' she said truthfully, because, in spite of the wrinkles, new babies always had something special going for them.

'Would you like to hold him?' asked Mrs Loder.

'May I?'

Clare took the proffered bundle and gazed down at the tiny face. 'You're a lovely boy,' she whispered, partly because it was expected of her, partly because she was suddenly swamped with emotion. It was a truism that women became broody at the sight and feel of a new baby. 'What are you going to call him?' she asked, and, as she lifted her head to look at Mrs Loder, caught Tom's eyes fixed on her.

His blue eyes, dark now with something other than passion, held hers. 'Feeling broody?' he asked in his velvet voice.

His words and presence overwhelmed her. It was

almost indecent in front of a roomful of people to feel so utterly possessed by him. She tore her eyes away from his.

'Kevin,' the mother was saying. 'Kevin William.'

'How nice,' replied Clare, handing her back her son. 'Congratulations,' she said to the father, and, to both of them, 'Thank you for letting me see and hold your son. Goodbye for now; I'll be seeing you and Master Kevin again.'

Tom held the door open for her, but was called back by one of the nurses as he was about to follow her out.

'Duty calls,' he said ruefully, turning back. 'I'll tell you tonight what I thought of you in the role of mother with child.' His look, before he turned away, devoured her.

Basking in the warmth of his words and looks, she finished her round. She was bleeped as she was about to leave Maternity; someone was waiting to see her, and she hurried back to her office.

On the way she met Noel Jefferson, the Canadian paediatric registrar from the General, coming to officially check out the new arrival.

He surprised her by saying, 'Hadn't seen you for a while, Clare, until last night at the Friary; guess you were having something to celebrate.'

'I didn't see you, Noel, and I was just having dinner with friends—nothing special.' The last thing she wanted was the hospital grapevine buzzing with rumour.

'Really?' He looked genuinely surprised, but also rather sardonic. 'Sorry, must have got the wrong impression. I remember being lectured by old Sir Ralph in his resonant tones at good old Almas. Couldn't help overhearing him over the clash of cutlery—something about congratulations being in order, wasn't it?'

What bad luck, Clare thought, that he should have

been at the Friary last night. How much did he in fact hear, and how much was he guessing at? He was a notorious gossip, though otherwise a nice man.

'Oh, you must have heard Sir Ralph congratulating Bill Bennett on his appointment as junior consultant in his firm.'

'Yes, of course, that must have been it. Good old Bill, all he wants now is a devoted wife to fit into Sir Ralph's scheme of things.' He looked very alert and inquisitive.

'Well, I hope that he finds her,' she said firmly, realising that he was fishing for information.

'Yep, and soon.' He gave her an engaging grin. 'Well, I must be on my way and look at this infant, though, as Tom Hunter was on the spot, I guess it's only routine. Talented bloke; great to see him back in the good old UK where he belongs.'

He went in one direction and she in the other. Clare hoped that she had scotched any fanciful ideas that he might have garnered from last night's episode.

Back in her office she dealt with the visitor and then got stuck into the usual pile of paperwork. She was determined to get away by five and spend an hour getting ready for Tom. It was difficult not to be distracted, anticipating the delights of the evening before her. Training and discipline, however, enabled her to concentrate on her work.

She had almost finished by a quarter to five when Jacky knocked and breezed in.

'You artful old thing,' she said. 'You had an exciting evening yesterday, didn't you?'

Clare gazed at her friend in despair; obviously she had got together with Noel Jefferson and he'd lost no time in spreading his version of the events at the Friary.

She said cautiously, wondering just what Noel had inferred, and passed on, 'Well, it was exciting for Bill, and I was pleased for him, of course; he's worked hard for this consultancy.'

'Oh, come off it. That wasn't the most important event of the evening, so a little bird told me.'

'Your little bird being the General's paediatric registrar presumably. You know what a gossip he is, Jacky, and how prone he is to make up what he doesn't gather in facts. You should take everything that he says with the proverbial pinch of salt.'

Jacky shrugged and smiled rather maliciously. 'Even Noel's imagination isn't creative enough to conjure up an engagement out of the blue. I went to old Ralph's lectures too, you know, and I know how his voice carries.'

So Noel had heard practically everything—certainly enough to be sufficiently sure of himself to pass on the information. She wondered who else he might have spoken to. Perhaps he had been more discreet with other staff, only telling Jacky because she was an old friend. The sudden heart-stopping possibility came to her that he might have repeated his nonsense to Tom.

'When did you see Noel?' Clare asked, neither confirming nor denying Jacky's tale.

'A few minutes ago; he was in the car park.'

'On his way back to the General?'

'Presumably; he didn't say.' Jacky dropped her bantering air. 'Listen, Clare, I'm you friend; if it's true that you're engaged, surely you can tell me? I honestly don't see any need for secrecy or coyness. Bill's a nice bloke and a good catch—why are you being so cagey?'

'Because it's not true.'

Jacky looked as if she didn't believe her.

'Oh, I know what Noel overheard, but that was only Sir Ralph wrongly anticipating an engagement between Bill and me.'

Jacky still didn't seem convinced. 'Why should Sir

Ralph, who is nobody's fool, think that you were engaged?'

It was the big question. Without saying that Bill had led his chief falsely to believe this to be true, she couldn't properly explain. But she had no wish to complicate matters for him further. It was bad enough that he had to extricate himself from their phoney engagement to Sir Ralph, without letting the world and his wife know that he had exaggerated in order to confirm his appointment.

She said lamely, 'It was a misunderstanding.'

Jacky hooted with laughter. 'You're kidding— people don't misunderstand an engagement! Either you're for it or you're not.'

She gave Clare a hard, uncompromising look. So far she had been friendly and curious; now she was not. In a voice to match her expression she asked, 'If you're not engaged to Bill, are you interested in anyone else?'

Would it matter, wondered Clare, if she prevaricated, pretended not to understand what her friend meant? No point, she decided; Jacky would have to know some time.

'Yes.'

'Tom Hunter?'

'Yes.'

Jacky moved restlessly around the office. She turned, suddenly facing Clare across the desk. 'What about him? Does he feel the same way about you?'

She hesitated. Should she let Jacky know that Tom had all but declared himself? She decided against speaking for him; after all, he had said nothing firm about their relationship, only that he wanted her. 'That's for him to say.'

'He's only interested in a bit of fun on the side. He's no intention of settling down. You're not in his league, Clare; you'll only get hurt.'

'And you won't?'

'I'll admit that he's the first man I've had any interest in for a long time. But I'm experienced; I can still pull out of it if necessary with no more than superficial burns.'

'Look, this isn't getting us anywhere. I don't like talking about Tom like this. I love him. I'm available if he wants me. You must do whatever you think is right if you want him too.' Clare felt better once she had said it. At last it was out in the open—the way she felt about Tom. After weeks of uncertainty it was a relief to speak her mind and be honest with herself.

Jacky gave a wolfish sort of grin. 'Throwing down the gauntlet! Well, it makes a change—two women declaring themselves over a man instead of the other way about.' She extended a hand across the desk. 'May the best woman win,' she said.

'This is all very theatrical,' said Clare, rather embarrassed by Jacky's words and gesture. But she took her friend's hand and shook it firmly. 'Love and war,' she said jokingly.

'You bet,' replied Jacky seriously.

While she was getting showered and changed, ready for her evening with Tom, Clare wondered if Noel had said anything to him about the events at the Friary restaurant. The first thing she must do when he arrived was to put him in the picture completely. He would be the one person who must know the whole truth about Sir Ralph's announcement, even if it did make Bill look devious. Nothing was going to spoil her future, long or short, with Tom.

Once she had made up her mind to do this, she was able to relax and enjoy dressing to please him. It hadn't mattered before what she wore, but now she wanted to put on something especially for him. A pity she hadn't been able to go out to buy a new outfit for the occasion. That would come later. Anyway, it wasn't difficult to find something that would be new to him. Their outings had been few and far between, something, hopefully, that would be remedied in the future. He was due to remain at the hospital for at least another month as relief MO, and she would make sure that they made the most of it.

She had no idea where they were going for the evening, or how long the evening would last—all night, perhaps! She thrilled at the prospect of the delights ahead, and simultaneously chided herself for behaving like a lovesick schoolgirl. She remained determined that on this occasion she was not going to back off; nor would she allow him that privilege, however noble he might feel.

It was unlikely that they would spend the evening at the lodge, where they would be a target for prying eyes, but Tom had suggested that it would be somewhere quiet. She fished out of her wardrobe a simple white cheesecloth shift dress with boot-lace straps. A wide, shiny patent-leather belt dressed it up, but could easily be removed to produce the casual look. White high-heeled strappy sandals would look right in any setting, and teamed up well with a multi-coloured draw-string bag capable of looking carefree or sophisticated.

Not much make-up—she remembered him saying that she didn't need it—but lashings of her favourite rose perfume.

'You smell nice,' Tom said, arriving sharp at six as promised. 'And you look like a fantastic and beautiful child.' He flicked her fringe of fair hair. 'I especially like this, but you can take off the à la mode belt, my love—we're going to dine alfresco.'

'Oh, a barbecue; sounds great!' Out in the open, she

thought; no chance of intimacy—had he purposely arranged it so?

'Not all the evening.' He grinned as he gave her a sideways look that set her heart pounding. 'You must be patient, dear girl, and see what Daddy's arranged for you.'

He was very mature, sophisticated and pleased with himself. She hoped that he wasn't going to emphasise their age difference—he'd hinted at it before.

She watched his lean, brown, long-fingered hands on the wheel and shivered at the prospect of being seduced by them.

'You can't be cold, darling,' he said, smiling. He knew, of course, what her thoughts and feelings had been, and she blushed with a mixture of embarrassment and pleasure. She was glad that he knew. Why try to hide her feelings. . .why not, for once in her tidy, proper life, give herself up to pure enjoyment?

She returned his smile. 'I'm so looking forward to tonight. I've got the morning off so, from my point of view, there's no rush.'

'I know, I checked the list in your office,' he said, and added with a chuckle, 'I do believe you're propositioning me, Sister.' Then, his voice very low and husky, he murmured, 'I hope to make it very special for you, my love. I've arranged cover for myself for the morning, so we've all the time in the world.'

Clare sighed with happiness and sat back to enjoy the rest of the drive.

They made only desultory conversation, remarking on the wonderful weather and the beauty of the sun on the water. A meaningless dialogue. Both wanted to speak of love but couldn't find the words. Occasionally they touched each other. He would take his hand from the wheel and place it over hers, and she would lightly caress his arm or his thigh. The electricity between

them was phenomenal. Clare felt his body pulling at
her like a magnet. It was wonderful, exhilarating, and
a little frightening all at the same time.

Their journey took them mostly along the coast
road, but after about half an hour they turned inland,
following the estuary of the river. Finally they turned
again along a small tributary of the Adron, and Tom
drove between white gateposts into a clearing in a
copse of trees.

'Dad's retreat,' he said, pointing to a path through
the trees. He took her hand. 'It's quite a surprise.'

It was certainly that. At the end of the path through
the small wood they found themselves by the water's
edge, and there, floating high in the water but tethered
firmly to the bank, was an elegant houseboat. It was
painted white and green, and looked quite large. There
was a gangplank with rails, leading from the bank to
the boat.

'Let's go aboard,' said Tom. He turned suddenly and
scooped her up into his arms. 'Shall we call the
gangplank our threshold?' he asked, his head bent to
look down into her face so close to his.

'That's only for brides,' she said.

'Can we not stretch it to include our first night of
pre-nuptial bliss?'

'Pre-nuptial?'

'That's what I said.'

She asked in a trembling voice, 'Is this by way of
being a proposal, or have I got it all wrong?'

'No, darling, you've got it right. I've had my reasons
for not committing myself or you to a closer relationship, but they were blown away this afternoon in
Maternity. Seeing you holding that new baby made me
realise that my fears were groundless, or that they can
be overcome.'

'Fears?'

'I'll tell you of them some time; it was a question of fears and superstition going hand in hand.'

'I can't imagine you being superstitious.'

'Too long living in the East; it colours one's judgement and isn't always wrong.' Suddenly he became impatient. 'Well, what is it to be—over the threshold, or have you any reservations, any hidden dark and mysterious reasons for not committing yourself?'

She hesitated a fraction, recalling the non-engagement to Bill that she must tell Tom about, but now was not the time. She pushed the unwelcome thought away, and looked up the length of the gangplank. 'It's a long threshold,' she said, 'but, if you can make it without getting a hernia, I'm game.'

He threw back his head and gave a great shout of exultant laughter. 'There speaks the perfect nurse. What a treasure will be mine when we marry.'

He carried her up to the deck of the houseboat as if she were a feather, and then down half a dozen steps to a cabin.

He set her down then, and she looked around with interest.

'Main cabin,' he explained. 'Master bedroom's in here.' He opened a door at one end. 'Of course, I can give you a guided tour now, if you like. But I don't think that I can wait much longer, my darling.'

'Nor I,' she replied.

His blue eyes blazed down at her. 'You're sure? No hang-ups, no dark secrets?'

She shook her head. 'We've both waited too long.'

'Oh, yes,' he said huskily, 'we have.'

He took her hand again and drew her through the narrow door to the bedroom. A huge double bed took up much of the space.

He sat down on the edge of the bed and pulled her gently down on to his knees. 'I've loved you,' he said softly, 'from the moment you came into your office in the middle of a thunderstorm. Poor darling, you had a migraine coming on.' He kissed her forehead. 'But I'm so afraid of hurting you, my love.'

'You can only do that by not loving me.'

'Never that.'

'Then what are we waiting for?' She began to unbutton his shirt, and fumbled a little. 'I'm not very good at this,' she whispered.

'What about all the patients you've undressed?'

'That was quite different.'

'I'm glad to hear it.' He smiled and nuzzled her neck and then put up a hand and slipped the boot-lace straps of her dress from her shoulders. He kissed her bare breasts. 'Beautiful,' he muttered. Her dress slipped to her hips. He stood her up and it slithered to the floor, leaving her standing in the briefest of briefs. His long fingers slid them down over her slender hips and he kissed her taut abdomen and stroked her thighs.

Clare held her breath as he rose and stood in front of her, stripped off his shirt and unselfconsciously dropped his trousers and shorts to the floor. He gathered her into his arms and pressed her against his hard, lean body, kissing her face and neck and then her lips. Her mouth opened under the onslaught and his tongue probed and pushed with ever-increasing passion. At last he lowered her gently on to the bed and knelt over her.

'No doubts?' he asked in a low throaty voice.

'None.'

He lowered himself on to her and she arched herself to meet him.

Their coming together was all that she hoped it might be. They made love several times and each time it seemed more satisfying, more complete. In the early hours of the morning they got up and made a huge pot of tea and a mound of toast and scrambled eggs. Tom explained that a Mrs Grant, who kept the boat tidy for his father, had stocked up the fridge and larder at his request.

'Thank God for Mrs Grant,' said Clare. 'I'm ravenous.'

'And I,' said Tom. 'Nothing like making love to give one an appetite.'

They went on deck to watch a pink, pearly dawn materialise out of the summer mist and then returned to bed and more gentle lovemaking.

Later in the morning they sat over coffee, making quiet conversation, and for the first time Tom seemed willing to tell her something of India and his personal life there.

'Why have you been so moody,' Clare asked, 'seeming to want me one minute and reject me the next? Is it because you've not been well, or connected with something else that happened to you?'

'Both, my love. I was afraid of lumbering you with a semi-invalid until recent tests showed that I'm really on the mend, so that was one problem out of the way. But there has been another, a more difficult reservation which I've had to come to terms with. I've had long-term liaisons with two other women, Clare.' He hesitated, gave her a smile and a kiss. 'Both were entered into for reasons other than passionate love, but lovingly, if you can appreciate the distinction.'

She nodded; she was rather surprised to hear that there had been two serious relationships in his life and was glad that his feelings were differently involved.

'I married one, and would have married the other had it been possible. I told you I wasn't a one-night-stand merchant. Deep down I'm quite conventional, and socially stable at heart.' He smiled and took her hand, squeezing her fingers gently; he could see that his announcement about being married had shaken her.

'I married Anne years ago, just after we took our finals. We were at med school together, and so was my best friend, the man she loved. They were mad about each other and wanted to get married against both their families' wishes. They thought that they were too young. The hospital authorities weren't too thrilled about it either.'

'So what happened?'

A bleak look passed over Tom's face. He looked incredibly sad. It was Clare's turn to squeeze his hand.

'Andy died as the result of a car crash. The three of us were out together. I was driving, Anne and he were in the back. A run-away lorry hit the back of the car. Both Anne and Andy were badly injured. I had hardly a bruise.'

'And you felt guilty?'

'How did you know?'

'It's written all over your face.'

'Well, I did escape unharmed. But I soon realised that I shouldn't feel guilty about the accident, just do what I could to help Andy and Anne.'

'But Andy didn't survive.'

'He took three weeks to die. It was agony watching, being unable to do anything. I think I learned more about medicine during that time than during my training.'

'How long did Anne take to recover?'

'About six weeks, during which time she discovered that she was pregnant.'

'And that was when you decided to marry her?'

'Yes, though our need was mutual. We were both totally shattered by Andy's death. His family were marvellous; they seemed to understand our reasons for marrying, though they didn't know about Anne's being pregnant. Her family were just so grateful that she was alive that they gave us their blessing. My parents seemed to understand too, but I had the feeling that Dad knew about Anne. He's always been very perceptive.'

'Where did you live after you were married?'

'India—we got a joint post, assisting for a year with a mission. There was great encouragement then for newly qualified medics to round off their training by doing a stint in the Third-World countries. We wanted to get away from Britain and memories of Andy, and Anne wanted to have her baby abroad.'

'So what happened—did she have the baby successfully?'

'No, she died a few months later in a flash flood, ironically attending an Indian woman in labour.'

'Oh, how dreadful for you, darling!'

'Made grimmer by the fact that I should have been attending the woman, but was held up in one of the outlying villages by the same flood that drowned Anne.'

'What did you do after that?'

'Finished my stint in a village not far from Calcutta, came home, worked in London, Glasgow, and Edinburgh to qualify in surgery as well as medicine, then returned to India.'

'Where you met your Indian lady?'

'Yes, though that was only three years ago.'

'Tell me about her.' Clare felt that she'd had almost enough of revelations for one day, but at the same time wanted to know everything that Tom was prepared to reveal about his past.

It was strange, sitting on the deck of an English houseboat on a typically English river on a sunny summer morning and hearing about life in a far-away tropical country. Except for Tom's distress at times

when he was narrating his story, she felt that she might
have been listening to *Tales from the East*, or something similar.

'Indira was with the mission that I was sent to. She
was resisting the efforts of her family to marry her to a
man who had been chosen for her when she was a
child. For some reason she had been allowed a Western
education and training as a doctor, but then they
wanted her to resume the role of a typical Indian
woman. I would have married her, but she wouldn't go
against her father's wishes to that extent, though she
was prepared to live with me and hope that the man
she was betrothed to would turn her down.' He stopped
and looked away into the distance.

'And?'

With difficulty he pulled himself back from his
reverie. 'I'll never know if she might have been successful. She died of the bug that I picked up about
eighteen months ago. She too was pregnant, although
I didn't know this until after her death.'

'Was it your child?'

'Oh, certainly; we were totally faithful to each other.'

'Oh, Tom, you've had a dreadful time.' She leaned
forward and kissed him on the cheek, and said softly,
'I'll try to make it up to you.'

His expression changed from sad to austere and
remote. He said bitterly, 'You mean you won't die on
me with or without child!'

'Tom. . .' She couldn't say more. She stared at him
in stunned silence.

He seemed suddenly weary, all the loving companionship that they had shared since last night drained
from him. He looked at her as if she were a stranger.

'I'm sorry,' he apologised, but it was in a cold,
distant voice. 'That wasn't fair. But I'm sure you now
appreciate my reluctance to get too close to a woman.

I'm bad news, Clare, a rotten lover long-term. I bring nothing but disaster to my partners.'

She thought, He's regretting having half committed himself to marriage. Out loud she said, 'What nonsense; that's sheer supersitition! I'm surprised that you can think such things.'

'They wouldn't think it strange out East.'

'But you're not out there now, and you're an educated Englishman who should know better.'

'I'm half a Scot.'

'A canny, hard-headed Scot. . .that makes it worse!'

'We are also credited with being a bit fey, you know.'

Clare got up. She said stonily, 'You don't have to go to such lengths to back out of your near-proposal.'

Tom looked genuinely astonished. 'Nothing,' he said firmly, 'was further from my mind.'

He stood up and walked towards her. She thought that he was going to fold her in his arms, and make everything all right, but he simply took her hands and held her at arm's length.

'I know it must all seem a nonsense to you, safe and so very secure in civilised Sussex, but I can't rid myself of the idea that somehow I bring disaster to any woman that I get close to.'

'What if I'm ready to take that risk?'

'I might take advantage of you.'

'Then will you do that, please? Because anything else is unthinkable. I love you, Tom.'

'And I you,' he said, kissing her gently but without passion. He was suddenly brisk. 'We'd better get going soon; duty calls.' He was smiling, trying hard to return to normal.

'I'm ready when you are.'

They spent a few minutes tidying up before setting off on their return journey.

The drive through the sunlit summer countryside was

uneventful. They didn't talk much, each immersed in
private thought. Clare was more bothered by Tom's
disclosures and his attitude than she cared to admit.
The delights of the night and early morning had almost
been destroyed for her.

They arrived back at the hospital just before twelve.

'No sense in trying to deceive the natives,' Tom said,
taking her arm and grinning hugely as a nurse eyed
them with obvious curiosity as they arrived at Clare's
flat. 'Do you mind?'

For some reason, Clare found it irritating that he
seemed back to normal. She wished she could brush
aside the last hour or so as readily as he appeared to
have done.

'I've not much choice, though I wish. . .'

'What do you wish?'

'I don't know.'

'You seem uneasy.'

'Do I? You must be mistaken.' She shrugged and
shivered. 'Someone walking over my grave,' she said
by way of explanation.

'Yes,' replied Tom, giving her a hard look.

He escorted her to the door of her flat, and kissed
her gently. 'Thanks for everything, my darling,' he said
as he left. 'See you on duty.'

Suddenly she remembered Bill and the ridiculous
muddle over his announcement of their non-engagement. She had to tell Tom now, before he heard it
elsewhere. Even if their marvellous night together had
ended as it had, and he seemed to be back-tracking on
his romantic proposal, she had to be honest with him.

'Tom, wait.'

He paused, his hand on the car door. She thought
that he looked impatient. 'Yes?'

'You might hear a silly rumour that's going around

about me and Bill Bennett,' she blurted out. 'It's not true. I can explain everything.'

To her astonishment, he shrugged.

'Oh, that,' he said dismissively. 'Noel mentioned it when he came to check out the new baby yesterday. In fact he couldn't wait to pass it on. It was obviously not true, or you'd have told me.' He opened the car door and seated himself. 'Bye, darling.' He raised a hand in salute and cruised slowly down the drive.

What an extraordinary man, she thought; he had believed in her totally, never doubting her for a moment, even after Noel's exposé of the events at the Friary.

She let herself into the flat to get ready for duty.

CHAPTER ELEVEN

CLARE relieved Jacky, who had been covering for her, at two o'clock. She wondered how her friend would react after their strange confrontation the day before. In fact she found her subdued and not looking well.

'You've got a temperature,' she said, looking at Jacky's flushed face. She took her pulse. 'And that's way over normal. Come on, sit down and I'll take your temp properly.'

The fact that Jacky didn't protest was significant. Her temperature was nearly thirty-nine degrees centigrade.

'Bed for you, old thing. I'll let the home manager know that you're on the way. You know the drill: lots of fluids and paracetamol, and if you haven't improved in a couple of hours I'll get old Doc Hunter to have a look at you.'

'Don't you mean young Dr Hunter?' asked Jacky with some of her usual spirit. 'Would you say that that was a Freudian slip inspired by wishful thinking?'

Clare felt herself blushing. She had momentarily forgotten that Tom was filling in for his father, but refused to consider that there was any deeper meaning than forgetfulness in her remark.

'Nice try, Walsh,' she replied with a smile, 'but it won't wash; I simply forgot.'

'I thought that he might be on your mind after last night.'

'Last night?' she said innocently, knowing that her friend might guess, but couldn't know for certain that she and Tom had spent it together. No way was she

going to give herself away to anyone, least of all Jacky.
'Go on, take yourself off to bed; I'll pop over later on.'

She picked up the phone and dialled the staff quarters to warn the manager of Sister Walsh's arrival. Jacky left and Clare watched her walk slowly up the drive to the flats, her back sagging, looking very dejected.

Almost before she had disappeared Sister Thorpe arrived at the office.

'One of my students has got a raised TPR and looks ghastly,' she said. 'She lives at home and I'd like to send her off duty; do you think someone could take her?'

'Oh,' said Clare flatly, 'it looks as if we're in for a mini-epidemic of something—summer flu perhaps.' She told the surgical sister about Walsh.

'Well, bang go my days off, I would think,' said Di Thorpe in a resigned voice. 'What do you want me to do about the other staff—alert them about reporting if they feel off-colour?'

'Not yet; for heaven's sake, don't let's give them ideas. After all, these two incidents might be isolated. We won't broadcast the possibility yet, but I'll have a word with all seniors to be on the look-out, and let Tom Hunter know. He'd better check your nurse before she goes off for the record, but tell her that she must see her own GP when she gets home.'

'Right, I'll get cracking. And don't worry about Women's Surgical, Clare; we'll manage. Thank God Sorrell's on holiday, so no patients for him, and no take-in tomorrow.' She beamed at Clare, who gave her a grateful smile. What a tower of strength she was.

So was Tom when she phoned to arrange for him to examine the student and Jacky. He must have been alone in the doctor's office, for he called her darling and sounded very solicitous.

'You're right to start taking precautions, my love,' he told her in a quiet reassuring voice, making her sound very precious. 'But let's hope that two sick nurses don't indicate an epidemic, or at least have given us enough warning to take avoiding action. I'll be over to see you as soon as I've examined these two.'

She felt guilty at being pleased to hear him refer to Jacky so casually, and felt that his attitude had salvaged something from their rather mixed morning.

Relatives of two night nurses rang in within a few minutes of each other to report flu-like symptoms and notify that they would be absent from duty. There was now little doubt that a flu bug of some sort was going around.

Tom called in at her office as promised and she gave him the news of the other two suspect cases.

'Well, there doesn't seem much doubt that we're in for something. Better put a stop to admissions, I think, my dear. You're going to be hard-pressed as things are without more patients. I'll get in touch with Brian Oats at the General and get his official OK as senior MO.'

'Do you think that we need to stop admissions yet? We've only a few ENT patients due in tomorrow for Mr Lewis; they'll only be warded for twenty-four hours, and then there are a couple of people for Women's Medical. We've only four staff off, and I can probably cover those from the agency.'

Tom was surprised. 'My darling girl, what are you thinking of? Four off now, and if, as seems highly likely, we've got a flu bug then you can double that up in the next twelve hours at least. However willing, neither you nor the other staff can cope with extra work, and I wouldn't allow you to try. No way are you going to get over-tired and more prone to infection if I can help it,' he added fiercely, giving her a lovely smile and reaching over the desk to pat her hand.

It was wonderful to be so protected, but she was still reluctant to stop admissions. Matron Stone had somehow managed with reduced staff on a similar occasion last winter; surely Clare could match her effort?

But whatever arguments she put forward Tom was adamant about keeping patient numbers down. He finally convinced her by reminding her that the patients themselves might fall victim to the bug—a frightening possibility.

There was no difficulty in convincing Brian Oats that admissions should be cancelled. Apparently several people had already gone sick at the General.

'Will you send a clerk over to sort out the paperwork here and make the necessary contacts?' Tom asked. 'Clare's got enough to do without having to cope with admin chores as well.' Apparently Brian agreed, for Tom put down the receiver looking pleased with himself. 'All fixed,' he said. 'Now let's get a plan of action together.'

They decided that all staff who had not had flu jabs should be given them. It might save one or two falling by the wayside, although it was a bit late in the day to hope for wide immunity. Probably the vaccine they had wouldn't cope with the current variety anyway, but it made sense to try.

The next week or so was exhausting for the staff who didn't succumb to the virus, as they were doing extra work covering for colleagues. Fortunately Jacky Walsh and one of the students who'd gone sick the first day were only slightly affected and returned to work after a few days. But later victims seemed to have contracted a more virulent strain and took longer to recover. Miraculously only three patients picked up the infection, and then not severely.

'Well,' said Tom, one afternoon ten days after the

epidemic had commenced, sitting in Clare's office and drinking his third mug of tea, 'the gods seem to be keeping watch over our flock. No fresh staff cases today, and the three patients on the mend. Soon be back to normal.'

'I shall sleep for a week when we are,' said Clare, yawning and stretching.

'Not if I'm around you won't!' retorted Tom, pretending to leer horribly. 'Do you realise, my darling, that we haven't been together since the houseboat, and I've scarcely been able to snatch one of these?' He leaned across and kissed her soundly but not passionately. 'I'm running out of steam,' he said dolefully, making her laugh.

'I dare say you'll recover, given a brief rest.'

'You bet!'

They smiled at each other lovingly. All the prickles and doubts that had assailed them on that morning after their night together had faded away. Working close together as they had over the past ten days had had a unifying effect. They had talked in the small hours of one morning, when Clare was covering a night duty, of their feelings for each other.

'I feel as if I have known you always,' said Clare.

'Yes,' agreed Tom, 'I've never experienced anything like this before. Do you think that it can be "That Old Black Magic Called Love"?'

'It's just possible,' she laughed.

His blue eyes darkened and he was about to come round the desk when they were interrupted by a nurse phoning from one of the wards.

Tom grinned tiredly. 'Just as well; I don't think I could have done justice even to kissing you—the spirit is willing but the flesh just ain't up to it, I'm afraid, my darling.'

They had laughed and gone to check on the patient the nurse was worried about.

It was surprising how often they had laughed together over the last ten days. Fighting fatigue and the occasional crisis that had arisen among the flu-stricken staff had triggered off their complementary sense of humour. Their joy in each other's company had deepened on this account. A sense of humour was one of the necessary ingredients Clare's father always stressed to his parishioners for a happy marriage. She thought how right he was.

Thinking of her father reminded her that at some point she must introduce Tom to her parents. But it was important to choose the right moment. She and Tom had talked of the strength and depth of their love during the night watches, but no further mention had been made of marriage.

Not that she any longer doubted Tom's word on the matter; he'd made it abundantly clear that he wanted a conventional relationship. What she wasn't sure of was *when*! He had vague plans for joining a friend who had a general practice in the Highlands for a period. The practice had connections with the mountain-rescue service, which was one of the attractions for him.

'Since I've been advised not to return to the tropics, at least for some time, I might consider the other end of the spectrum—the snowy wastes of Scotland. What do you think, love—would you like to live in the wild north?'

As so often these days, before she could answer they were interrupted by a call to attend to a patient. Clare had wanted to tell him that she would live happily in any part of the world if he was there, and determined that she would do so at the first opportunity.

Now at last it looked as if the emergency was coming to an end. They could breathe again. Enough senior staff were back on duty for her to consider taking a day off.

It was the twelfth day after the outbreak of flu.

'Will you be able to get a day off soon?' Clare asked Tom.

They were taking tea in her office after finishing the first almost normal round for nearly a fortnight.

Tom looked up from the prescription pad that he was signing. 'Is that an invitation to dalliance?' he asked, grinning like a schoolboy.

Claire tried to look prim. 'I thought you might like to come home and meet my parents,' she replied, dimpling with pleasure at the thought.

He didn't hesitate. 'I thought that you would never ask, dear girl. I should love to meet your family.'

'Perhaps the day after tomorrow. If we leave early we can get there by mid-morning and not have to leave till fairly late in the evening.'

'Great. There won't be any problem with surgical cover; I'll have to sound out several GPs for cover for their medical beds, but things are quieter now so I'm sure that I'll find someone to cope.'

'I'll phone Mother and tell her to expect us, if that's all right with you.'

Their eyes locked across the desk.

He said huskily, 'Everything's all right with me, my darling, if you're sure and happy.'

She flushed with pleasure. 'Oh, Tom, I'm very happy.'

She phoned her mother that evening to put her in the picture.

'Tom, Tom Hunter. . .he hasn't by any chance got a father or uncle who is a Roland Hunter, has he?'

'Yes, Mother, his father is Roland Hunter; I've told you about him before: he's the resident medical officer, but he's been ill and his son has taken over for him for a while.'

'Are you sure that you mentioned Roland Hunter before, dear?'

'Yes, positive, when I first took up my contract here about six months ago. Why?'

'I think that I was at school with his wife Natalie. She married a Roland Hunter doing medicine.'

'That was the name of his late wife.'

'Oh, dear; she's dead, then.'

'Yes, Mother.'

'What a pity. We were quite good friends at school. I would have enjoyed getting reacquainted with her.'

'Well, it's her son whom I'm bringing to meet you and Father the day after tomorrow. You will be there, won't you?'

'The day after tomorrow,' repeated her mother vaguely. 'Perhaps you'd better confirm with Rosie.'

Mrs Silk—Rosie—who had looked after them all for as long as Clare could remember, came on the phone.

'Your mother's in the middle of a picture,' she explained, knowing that Clare would understand that that accounted for her parent's vagueness. 'Do I understand that you are at last bringing home a *man*?' she asked in capital letters.

Clare gave her a brief résumé of her relationship with Tom.

'Oh, Clare, I'm so happy for you. . .can't wait to meet him, and I know that goes for your ma and pa too, though it'll take a while for it to sink in with them. You know how they are.'

Clare laughed; she did indeed know how vague both her parents were, though it didn't in any way diminish their love or the security they offered. In fact when her mother, who was a considerable artist, was not working on a picture, she was a different person—almost practical, and a super cook. Her father remained rather unworldly much of the time, though he somehow managed to be 'with-it' as well. Even his young parishioners found him easy to talk to.

She and Tom were able to take time off to go to the Castle Arms for a drink that evening. They sat at one of the tables in the garden behind the inn.

It was heaven to be free of their commitments after the hectic time they'd had recently. Clare lifted her face to the evening sun and sighed with pleasure. Tom slid an arm along the back of the bench and stroked the back of her neck.

'Oh, that's lovely,' she murmured. 'Don't stop. I love you touching me.'

He chuckled. 'I can think of more interesting places to——'

'Tom, behave yourself!' she interrupted, blushing and looking round to see if anyone might have heard what he'd said.

He laughed again and moved closer so that their thighs were touching.

'You blush delightfully, my darling.'

She gave him an imploring look.

'OK. I'll behave.'

'I phoned home this afternoon,' she said primly. 'My parents are looking forward to meeting you.'

His eyes were full of love and laughter. 'Are you trying to remind me how eminently respectable your folks are?'

'Not at all,' she replied haughtily, giving him a cool look, trying to ignore the sensuous motion of his fingers on the back of her neck. 'I just wanted you to know that our visit is arranged.'

She repeated the substance of her telephone call to

home, and how it was Rosie who'd really got things sorted out.

'Your parents sound delightful,' he said, 'and how nice that your mother knew mine at one time. And she's a professional painter—fantastic. What medium does she work in?' he wanted to know.

Clare remembered then that at almost their first meeting he had said that he enjoyed painting as a hobby, though no mention of it had been made since. 'Of course, you paint too. How lovely; you and Mother will have a lot to talk about. I am so looking forward to going home and introducing you to everyone.'

He said softly, teasing her with his eyes, 'You were going to go home weeks ago, remember, using it as an excuse not to go out with me?'

It seemed a lifetime ago, not just a few weeks since they'd met, so close had they grown to each other.

He took her hand and ran his thumb up and down the inside of her wrist. 'Your radial pulse is going like mad,' he whispered, his warm breath lifting tendrils of hair above her ear. 'Shall we finish our drinks and go back to the lodge, where we can say goodnight properly?'

Clare hesitated. 'Someone's bound to see us. Is it wise, do you think? After all, you are the MO and you know how people talk. Even if you don't mind, is it fair to your father?'

Tom looked surprised. 'Oh, come on, love; you don't really mind what people think, do you? I thought we'd established that you haven't any hang-ups now that things are settled between us. Everyone will know soon enough that we've got a serious relationship going.'

Perhaps she was suffering from the effects of being over-tired, or perhaps it was because he spoke of a relationship and not marriage, but his reply irritated her.

'That's all you men think of,' she said in a low bitter tone. 'Sex.'

He moved slightly away from her along the bench. 'Well, I have to admit that after nearly a fortnight my normal instincts and your beautiful body are influencing my thoughts in that direction.' He smiled at her in the gentle, loving way that usually bowled her over.

This evening she couldn't respond and she didn't know why, though she knew that he was trying to tease her out of her sudden bad temper. How could things change between them in a matter of minutes? Was it partly because she was excited by the thought of being made love to by him, and she felt guilty? But why feel guilty now? As he'd rightly said, she'd discarded any inhibitions that she'd had during that wonderful night on the houseboat.

She said in a hard little voice, 'You can't even bring yourself to mention the word marriage, can you? We're just a relationship, like the one you had with Indira.'

The words appalled her the moment they were out. She would have done anything to recall them.

His fingers tightened round his glass, the knuckles turned white, but he answered in an equable voice.

'My dear girl, I thought that I'd made myself clear on the matter. We agreed that a loving relationship was what we both wanted. Does it matter if it's called marriage? Some of those are not worth the paper they're written on.'

'So you don't want to get married?' She grabbed her shoulder-bag from the table and stood up. 'I just want you to be honest with me.' She stood in front of him, grey eyes smouldering. 'Jacky was right, after all; she said that you just wanted some fun on the side, and she was right. But, Dr Tom Hunter, I'm not that piece of fun. I've not got the morals of an alley-cat, and you need someone who has.'

Even as she said it and moved away through the tables as fast as she was able she knew that it wasn't true. Tom might not be ready for marriage, but he wasn't lecherous and he honestly thought that he loved her, and even that he was in love with her.

Jacky was only partly right about his attitude to sex, though she couldn't know that the reasons for his seemingly casual approach was the result of two tragedies in his life. But she was accurate in her assessment of his needs and also about the hurt that he might unwittingly inflict on Clare herself.

On the walk back to the hospital, she admitted to herself that she couldn't accept, as she had imagined, any relationship with Tom other than marriage. It followed that, as he didn't want this, there could be nothing between them at all. She must go away as soon as her work allowed. In the meantime she must avoid him like the plague. He had only to touch her, look into her eyes, or speak loving words in that velvet-soft voice of his, and she was bereft of all logical thought and action.

As she turned into the drive she became aware that he was following her. She took to her heels and started to run. She would be finished if he caught up with her and tried to plead his cause as she was sure that he would.

She reached the lodge, and was surprised to see the downstairs rooms ablaze with lights shining out through the summer dusk.

'Clare,' a familiar voice called, and she turned her head to see old Dr Hunter standing in the porch.

She stopped running and turned towards the garden gate. 'What on earth are you doing back?' she asked, surprise making her ask the obvious and momentarily overlook her own present situation. 'Are you all right?'

'Fine—that's why I'm back. Had enough of convalescence; I'm in great shape.' He had walked down the garden path to greet her, and now eyed her up and down in some surprise. 'Are you supposed to be jogging? You don't look dressed for the part.'

At that moment Tom appeared, walking very fast round the bend in the drive. He stopped suddenly when he saw Clare and his father in conversation.

'Dad, what on earth are you doing back?'

'You tell him, Clare,' said Dr Hunter, looking keenly at both of them.

'He simply feels fit enough to work again,' she said, hoping that her voice gave nothing away to either man. Dr Hunter senior was already summing up the situation with great interest. She didn't trust herself to his sharp intuition, any more than she trusted herself to his son's charm.

Somehow she managed to extricate herself from further conversation, pleading tiredness and the desire for an early night. Part of this was at least true. She was exhausted, as were all the well staff, from overwork during the emergency, and longed for her bed. She knew, though, that she wouldn't sleep before exorcising the events of the evening from her mind.

Some time later, lying in bed, resigned to not sleeping, she went over and over the events, not only of the evening but of the period of time since she had met Tom. More than ever she was convinced that, however deeply her feelings were involved, his were only superficially engaged.

She had respected his fear of harming her because of what had happened to Anne and Indira. In spite of her being surprised that a man of education and intelligence could give way to superstition he had made it seem a genuine reason for initially keeping her at arm's length. Now she had reached the conclusion that, consciously or not, he was using his fear to avoid marriage.

She was trying desperately to get to sleep when the phone rang.

'Clare, I'm awfully sorry to disturb you,' Sarah Barnes's voice said quietly in her ear; Sarah was the senior night sister on duty, 'but we have a staff casualty.'

'Who, and what is wrong?' asked Clare briskly. She realised that she was glad of the interruption in her efforts to get to sleep.

'It's Roger Kenny, the third year student on Men's Surgical. He's more or less collapsed. Pulse rapid, tachycardia.'

'Phone Dr Hunter; I'll be with you pronto.'

She and Tom arrived together in the ward office, where Roger had been when he'd collapsed. Night Sister had done all the right things, putting him in a semi-reclining position on two chairs, loosening his tie and trousers, and covering him with a blanket. She'd moistened his lips with water, but had not given him anything by mouth. There was a resuscitation tray laid up for use if necessary.

'Fine,' said Tom. 'You couldn't have done more.'

'Look, Sarah, you get back on the wards, I'll stay with Dr Hunter. Phone and see if you can get an emergency replacement for Roger. There should be someone on the list willing to come on.'

'Right, will do. Thank God we've got Kate King on as Auxiliary here on Surgical. She's brilliant. I'm sure she can cope till I get more help.'

She went away to speak to the auxiliary, who was quietly going about her duties, as Clare could see through the ward window. Together she and Tom bent over Roger.

Tom said gently, 'I'm going to have a listen, see what's happening.'

He very carefully, and with great concentration, examined the student's chest. He listened, with eyes closed, to the sounds from the heart, his whole attention absorbed by what he was hearing through his stethoscope. He straightened up at last.

'Roger, you're fibrillating, as I'm sure you've guessed. Now, this may go away in a few hours or a few days, but it is more likely that you are going to need some long-term treatment. Sister. . .' he smiled fleetingly at Clare '. . .will arrange for you to go into a side-ward on Medical, and I'll give you an injection of propranolol before we move you. That'll make you feel more comfortable. In the morning we'll get the cardiac specialists to have a look at you, and see what they suggest. OK?'

'OK, Doc, whatever you say.' He closed his eyes wearily, and then opened them suddenly. 'Sister, can you let my mum know? She'll be worried if I don't get home as usual in the morning.'

'Don't worry about anything, Roger. I'll phone her myself, early in the morning, but let her have an undisturbed night if Dr Hunter agrees.' She looked questioningly at Tom. He hadn't mentioned Intensive Care, so she presumed that there was no critical element involved.

He nodded in reply to her unspoken question. 'That should be fine, Sister. No need to worry Mrs Kenny at this hour that her son is skiving off night duty.' He gave the young student one of his most reassuring smiles.

'I'm not for the mort yet, then, Doc?' asked Roger, trying to produce a shaky smile.

'Not for the next fifty years or so, I would think,' replied Tom.

Keith, the night porter, arrived with a wheeled stretcher. He helped Tom lift Roger on to the stretcher. He happened to be the same porter who had been on duty on the morning that the orderly had sustained a venous bleed after an injury to his leg.

Tom grinned at him. 'Do you make a habit of being around when staff come a cropper?' he asked, well aware that humour was the most reassuring commodity for the patient.

'Well, Doc, since you ask,' replied Keith, appreciating the situation with commendable acumen, 'I just looks at me horoscope and volunteers, like, for certain duties.' He gave Roger an engaging smile. 'C'mon then, Nurse, let's be having yer.'

Clare watched doctor, patient and orderly depart, before joining Auxiliary Nurse King in the ward, knowing that everything was under control on Men's Medical for receiving Student Nurse Kenny in the side-ward.

'Anything I can do to help, Nurse?' she asked in a whisper.

'All under control, Sister,' confirmed the auxiliary, and then asked, 'How's Roger?'

'More comfortable. Dr Hunter gave him an injection and he'll be looked after on Men's Medical till morning.'

'I'm so pleased,' said the middle-aged auxiliary. 'I hoped he wouldn't need intensive care. I suppose they hope to get him stabilised on Men's Med?'

'Probably, with luck. Thank you for getting Night Sister so promptly, Kate. You saved the day.'

Kate King shook her head. 'No, if anything it was the night that I saved.' She gave Clare an impish grin.

'Not that I did anything—it was Sister who did all the right things.'

'That's not quite the impression that I got, Kate.'

'Well,' Kate gave a shrug, 'you pick up bits and pieces after fifteen years or so on the job. You'd have to be a fool if you didn't.'

'Well, thanks anyway.'

Clare made her way to Men's Medical to see that Roger was settled in, and then checked with Night Sister that there was a relief on the way.

It was three o'clock when she at last found her way back to her flat and fell into bed, though not immediately to sleep.

Tom's face and his hands wielding the stethoscope kept coming between her and sleep. How kind, understanding and gentle he had been when examining Roger Kenny. How easily he had switched into the special relationship that bound all hospital staff together, uniting the porter, student nurse, herself and himself as doctor in a unit of caring professionals.

She tossed and turned, waiting for sleep to come.

Through exhaustion Clare at last fell asleep, but woke in the morning looking and feeling as if she hadn't closed her eyes all night.

She went on duty with a lump of sadness and despair in her chest and a thumping great headache. Somehow she got through her chores and fended off sympathy about how tired she looked by pleading a cold. She was on tenterhooks the whole morning, wondering when Tom would appear, but by lunchtime there had been no sign of him.

It was after lunch, a meal which she couldn't eat, that everything began to catch up with her.

Dr Hunter senior appeared at two o'clock. He knocked at her office door, entered at her invitation, and slapped an envelope down on her desk.

'From Tom: it explains why I'm doing the round and what his movements are for the next few days.' He looked very angry.

'You shouldn't get so worked up,' said Clare. 'It isn't good for you, and I'm not sure that you should be on duty.'

'Cleared with Brian Oats. Phone him if you want to, and I'm only worked up on your behalf, Clare.'

'It still isn't good for you,' she replied, trying to smile in spite of her headache. 'Anyway, it's nice to have you back.'

'You look pretty poorly, lass. What's up, apart from my boy giving you a hard time?'

'I'm all right, and he isn't giving me a hard time. Please, I'd rather not talk about it.'

'You're telling me not to be nosy. Fair enough; Tom said much the same, but he was anxious that you should read his letter.'

'Presently,' she said, restraining herself from tearing open the envelope. 'I'd better come with you on the round; there have been quite a few changes since you went away.'

The round took over an hour. Old patients who knew Dr Hunter wanted to renew acquaintance, and new ones make comparisons with his son.

The phone was ringing when they got back to Clare's office.

She picked up the receiver and announced, 'Deputy Matron Browning.'

'Clare,' said a familiar voice in her ear. 'How are things?'

'Matron Stone, what a surprise! How lovely to hear from you.'

'I'm coming back at the end of the week, ready for the fray and to give you some time off.'

'How marvellous. Are you sure that you're ready for work?'

'Well, I can't pretend that I'm ready for ward work, but a round or two and a chance to relieve you of the paperwork is well within my capabilities. It'll only be for three months anyway. I've decided to take early retirement.'

'Oh, no, you can't do that!' The idea of taking on the full-time job of matron was too daunting for words. Besides, Matron Stone was only in her mid-fifties; she'd go spare without a full working day to contend with.

'I felt that I had no option but to offer to retire when I heard the plans for the Cottage. No way could I go along with the changes that are planned.'

'What changes?'

'Oh, dear, hasn't anybody had the courtesy to tell you what is planned for the General and the Cottage?'

'No one's said a word.'

'Well, best that I don't either, at least until I see you in a few days' time. Hasn't Roland Hunter said anything?'

'He's only just got back from sick leave, you know, recovering from his heart attack.'

'Oh, yes, of course. How is he?'

Clare managed a smile across her desk to the doctor. 'He's in good form. Would you like to speak to him?'

To Clare's surprise she said no, but that she looked forward to seeing him on her return. She then rang off.

Dr Hunter surveyed her pale face. 'Marjorie has told you something that's upset you?' he asked.

'Surprised me would be more accurate.'

'She thought that you knew of the plans that are being made for the two hospitals?'

'Yes—how do you know?'

'I'm on the board. Why do you think I've come hot-footing it back from the best fishing I've had in years?'

'I thought it was because you had recovered.'

'Well. . .' he gave her a smile almost as heart-stopping as his son's '. . .that too, but I had this other reason.' He looked distressed. 'I can't believe that they haven't put you in the picture.'

'Nobody's said a word about changes.'

'It's bloody well not fair, my dear, and certainly wouldn't have happened had Rachel and I not both been away.'

'Oh, yes, Lady Rachel. . .she's in the Far East on some mission or other.'

'A grand lady; great worker for the poor and underprivileged.'

'Yes, I like her very much.' She took a deep breath, and asked, 'Dr Hunter, what's going on?'

'There's a move afoot towards amalgamation with the General. It'll be a great financial gain, especially with the new system of self-finance coming into force. The Cottage Hospital's charter allows for change where this is seen to be beneficial to the local community; I'm afraid the powers working against us can appear to prove this, though Rachel and one or two of us on the board see this as the thin edge of the wedge towards total integration with the General.'

'That's what Matron Stone meant about not being able to go along with the idea, then?'

'I should think so. And, Clare, unless you are prepared to accept all the changes proposed, I don't think that you can count on the position of matron being offered to you automatically, in spite of all that you've done while Marjorie has been off sick.'

'I see.' She felt cold and sick inside herself. Already grieving for what might have been between herself and Tom, she had now discovered that her work, hitherto her saving grace, was under threat. If Matron Stone couldn't stomach the machinations of the board, still less could she. It confirmed her tentative decision to resign.

'I shall resign at once,' she said, and was surprised when Dr Hunter didn't try to dissuade her.

He stayed to drink tea and discuss the patients and their treatment, but didn't mention the changes or Tom's letter again.

Jacky Walsh came in just after he left. She had been very quiet and rather distant with Clare since her attack of flu, though not unfriendly. Now she remarked in a solicitous voice that Clare looked off-colour.

'Yes, and I feel it,' replied Clare, to her colleague's surprise. She told her about Matron Stone coming back on duty in a few days' time and her own resolve to take some holiday due to her, but said nothing about the changes planned.

'Good idea,' said Jacky, 'and you're off tomorrow, aren't you? Doing anything special?'

Clare couldn't be sure if she knew that she and Tom had intended going to her home, but suddenly felt that it didn't matter anyway.

'I was going to go home, but I'm not feeling brilliant, so I might just take it easy in the flat or the garden.'

'Not going anywhere with Tom?'

'Probably not.' She tried to sound casual and uninterested. 'He's busy,' she invented.

Jacky seemed not to know what to make of her answer. 'Well,' she mumbled, 'have a nice day, anyway.'

'I certainly will,' replied Clare with more firmness and enthusiasm than she was feeling.

It was a relief when she was able to go off duty at five o'clock. She dragged herself up to her flat, feeling a million years old. Although it was early she poured herself a drink and went and sat in the garden in the afternoon sunshine to read Tom's letter.

For a long time she sat holding it unopened in her hand, both wanting to know and dreading to read what he had to say.

At last she tore open the envelope and started to decipher his appalling scrawl.

CHAPTER TWELVE

Tom's letter read:

Darling Clare,

I had hoped to rectify the disastrous events of yesterday evening, if not immediately, certainly at the first opportunity today. Unfortunately I've been asked to give an opinion on a patient suffering from a rare disease that I came across in India. When you read this I shall be in London, possibly for a few days, though I will try to get back some time tomorrow in the hope of seeing you, even if I have to return to town later.

It was most unfortunate that my father was at home when we got back yesterday evening. I'm sure that all could have been resolved then, had we been allowed the time and privacy. Suffice, at the moment, to say how sorry I am at the way things turned out. We were both tired after our marathon effort of the past week, which must have accounted for our needling each other so stupidly.

My dearest girl, I love you and want to marry you. There, I've said it, or rather written it, as plainly as I know how. I didn't realise that you thought I might be prevaricating until you showed how upset you were last night. All that rubbish that I spouted about long-term relationships being the same as marriage! We both know that they are not, unless they are inevitable under certain circumstances. Perhaps I have been wary of committing myself and found it convenient to use my fear of something going wrong as a reason when it was nothing but an excuse.

But all that is behind me, love. Come hell or high water I want you as my wife. Please overlook my ridiculous behaviour and say yes.

I love you.

Yours devotedly,
Tom.

PS If you see or contact your parents please convey my apologies for not showing up.

Clare sat with the letter open on her lap for a long time while tears splashed down on the page and some of the words ran together.

What was she to do? Tom was obviously sincere and so loving that it hurt. But he had seemed exactly the same during their night of loving and then changed the following morning. They had discussed her hang-ups, but ignored his because they seemed noble and self-sacrificing. Now even he was admitting that they were not solid reasons for holding back. But would this attitude endure? She needed someone to talk to.

Her mother in a practical mood would have made an ideal listener, but she was this moment in the middle of creating a picture. She would be no help. He father? No; as she and her brothers had grown up they had learned that their father was too removed from every-day events to be of much practical help. Love, sym-pathy and compassion, yes, and occasional flashes of what Rosie called 'divine wisdom', but the ability to direct their faltering steps, no. Odd that young and old in the parish found him a tower of strength where their problems were concerned, but his children sought solutions elsewhere.

Rosie would listen and offer sound advice, but for some reason Clare felt unable to discuss Tom with her. Had the man been any other than Tom she could have talked things through with Jacky. But that was out.

Jacky had too much of a vested interest in Tom to be able to give an impersonal view. In fact, the more she thought about it, the more she realised that only one person, Dr Hunter senior, would be the right person to advise her.

In spite of being Tom's father, he was the trained observer who could stand back and look at her problem with an impersonal eye. She telephoned the lodge.

'My dear Clare, do you want me to come to you, or will you come down here?' he asked, after she'd told him something of her dilemma.

'Might I come down to the lodge?'

'As soon as you like, my dear.'

She spent a few minutes on her face, ravaged by the tears she had shed over Tom's letter, and changed into a loose top and skirt before walking down to the lodge.

'We will eat first,' said Dr Hunter, taking no notice of the negative shake of the head, 'and talk afterwards.'

Amazingly she managed to eat some cold chicken and salad and a jacket potato oozing with butter.

'Now, tell me all,' commanded the doctor, ignoring her waving away of a brandy with her coffee.

It all came tumbling out. Her love for Tom, but her fears that he was only going along with her need for marriage to please her, not because he too wanted it. Without going into details, she told him of their night on the houseboat and his reaction the following morning. She told him too of the rapport that they had established through working together during the mini-epidemic. She found that she couldn't adequately explain last night and the way that Tom's physical need of her had affected her. She simply said, 'And it all came to a head last night, and now he's written me this lovely letter and asked me to marry him,' she added, unable to keep the surprise out of her voice, 'and in writing.'

'Well, you've got him for breach of promise should he choose to renege,' said Dr Hunter with a mischievous grin worthy of his son.

Clare didn't know whether to laugh or cry. 'Please,' she said in a broken little voice.

'My dear child. He loves you. That's abundantly clear. Does it matter if he's riddled with doubt from previous experiences? My poor boy—he's a sucker for the helpless. Can't you see that that's what made him enter into these two liaisons? But with you it is different: this is a relationship of equals, and he wants to rationalise it by marriage. It may have taken him a while to get there, but he knows that you won't settle for anything less, and is happy to be hooked.'

Clare thought that she might have preferred a better phrase than one that made her sound so predatory, but she accepted Dr Hunter's reasoning.

'So I should see him tomorrow if he comes, and make it up with him?'

'Certainly not! Not in that mealy-mouthed fashion, anyway. Play hard to get; see him, but make him work for seeing you.' He looked at her pretty, honest face and sighed. 'Well, you're not going to use feminine wiles to bring him to heel, are you?'

She smiled and shook her head. Already she was feeling better and able to cope with the situation.

'No,' she said, 'and I don't think that Tom needs me to do that, but I do need time. I'm an orderly person and don't like being rushed off my feet. Tom came along and turned my life upside-down. I need to reorientate myself.'

'That's my girl!' said Dr Hunter on a laugh. 'You make him be patient. He's had girls falling over him since he was a teenager—it'll do him good to have someone else set the pace.'

* * *

Surprisingly she slept well that night. Her talk with Dr Hunter senior had set her mind at rest. He was right—her future with Tom was secure—but she would put a temporary brake on their relationship. Slow things down so that she might have the time that she needed to savour the pleasure of being in love. It was another maxim of her father's that an old-fashioned period of courtship was, if not essential, an attractive and civilised beginning to marriage.

She could almost hear his melodious voice saying, 'It's a time for cherishing each other without the mundane problems of married life taking the shine out of your loving,' and, with his unexpected grasp of modern life, he would add, 'It's something I would recommend even before setting up house together; starting a long-term relationship, I think it's called.'

Clare thought how often her apparently unworldly father was right about life, even if she couldn't talk to him about her problems on a one-to-one basis.

She had phoned to say that she wouldn't be going home after all. Rosie accepted her reason, true anyway, that Tom had been called away.

'That's the only thing I've got against your marrying a doctor,' she'd said teasingly, 'the fact that he'll be away as much as he's home. But I dare say you think he's worth it.'

'Oh, I do,' Clare had replied fervently, thankful that this was now true and she didn't have to pretend with Rosie.

Tom would probably phone if he was able to get away, but, sticking to her resolve to be rather more detached, she decided not to sit around waiting for him. She would go out to lunch after doing chores around the flat and writing letters—her letters of resignation: one to the senior nursing officer at the General, one to Matron Stone as her immediate superior, and one to the Cottage Hospital Board as her official employers.

She felt light-headed and very happy. She was looking forward immensely to a few weeks' holiday from the time her resignation became effective. There were about three weeks owing to her as well as several days off not taken in the period she had been relieving Matron Stone.

With that lady back in a few days' time she could leave with a clear conscience. The hospital would have to rely on agency nurses, but, after the shabby way she had been treated, even her ultra-sharp sense of duty couldn't make her feel guilty.

The phone rang. It was Tom.

'Darling, you're not going to slam the receiver down on me, are you?'

She laughed with the sheer pleasure of hearing his voice. 'Of course not,' she replied softly.

'I can get down for a few hours this afternoon, but I must return this evening., I'll pick you up at the flat at about two-thirty and we'll talk ourselves through our problems, dear girl.'

'No,' she said, marvelling at herself being so firm. 'I'm going to lunch at the Castle Restaurant and then joining the tourists to look round the castle. I must see something of it before I leave.'

There was a moment's silence, and her heart thumped painfully. Had she gone too far. . .should she have agreed to a quiet tête-à-tête somewhere? After all, he'd written that lovely letter, just inviting her to fall into his arms, which was exactly where she would have liked to be. Perhaps his father was wrong about making him work for her favours. He'd learnt his lesson; surely she could leave it at that?

Tom chuckled in the lovely throaty way that he had.

'I believe you've been talking to Dad,' he said, 'and he's advised you to keep me on my toes.'

He was so right that it took her breath away. 'How did you guess?' she asked in a rather trembly voice.

'Because I know him as well as he knows me. We've a great rapport with each other. He's right, anyway, love. You deserve to be wooed.'

Clare, still feeling light-headed, shrieked with laughter. 'Wooed! How very old-fashioned!'

'But that's what you'd like, isn't it, my dearest girl? I shouldn't have tried to rush you off your feet. The houseboat affair was marvellous, but it's not really your style. You'll have to keep me in check until we're morally and officially married.'

The idea of playing it cool and hard to get grew less inviting every minute. If he'd walked through the door she'd have flung herself into his arms and begged him to seduce her. The thought of his body close to hers made her go hot all over, but she forced herself to say, with some semblance of normality, 'This phone call must be costing the earth in the middle of the morning. Do ring off, darling. I'll meet you at the castle—you can join me and the other hundreds of visitors in the baronial hall.'

Tom groaned theatrically. 'So I'm to be subjected to rectory economics as well as rectory morals. Shades of the Brontës.'

'It'll be good for you.'

'You'll be good for me,' he said, sounding quite serious. He rang off.

She was about to leave the flat when the postman arrived with the second delivery. There was one letter for her. She recognised Bill Bennett's writing immediately, and for one unpleasant moment she thought that his letter would spoil the day.

Then, with the new-found confidence that her talk

with Dr Hunter senior had given her, together with Tom's proposal, she realised that she was beyond Bill's reach. Whatever ingenious method of persuasion he might use, however he might try to make her feel guilty, she was now proof against his charm.

She'd had a few bad moments about him since her sharp rejection of his behaviour on the night of their dinner with the Foxes. She'd prayed that his consultancy was not at risk because he couldn't produce a wife. He really was a splendid paediatrician and should get the job on merit, not on marital status.

She tore open the envelope and prepared herself for the worst. The letter read:

Dear Clare,

I know that you will be pleased to learn that Sir Ralph has confirmed my appointment to his firm, in spite of the mess-up I made of things by implying that we were engaged. He's been marvellously understanding, though I suspect that Lady Fox has had a hand in the matter. Speaking of Lady Fox, she has just introduced me to her niece, Miranda. A smashing girl.

Sorry about the grief that I caused you over recent events. I'm really very fond of you, you know, and we could have made a go of things, had you been willing.

Anyway, I hear on the grapevine, via Jacky Walsh actually, that you and Hunter are pretty thick. Best of luck with the Hunter hunted, as it were.

Bill.

Clare smiled to herself as she screwed up the letter and threw it into the wastepaper basket. There had been no need to worry about Bill. He had regained his usual ebullience. She was glad about the consultancy; he would make a splendid paediatrician at top level and do wonderful things to further children's medicine. Good luck to him, and, she grinned to herself, good luck with the delicious Miranda! What a clever old thing Lady Fox was to sort out the problem of her husband's new assistant's non-married state.

Over lunch at the Castle Restaurant she thought about Jacky. Bill's comment about her set Clare thinking. It was strange that, having at one time thrown down the gauntlet, as she had put it, she had not pursued Tom. What had deflected her? The certainty that Tom wouldn't give in? She had seemed to back off during the virus epidemic. It was almost as if being physically sick had given her time to reflect on the matter. Perhaps seeing Clare and Tom working together in such harmony had convinced her that they belonged together.

Well, Clare decided as she finished her lunch, there's nothing I can do about Jacky, except wish her well. At least I won't be around for much longer to remind her that she lost Tom to me. She chided herself on being unbearably smug. She took herself off to the castle proper, joining the column of tourists waiting to cross the drawbridge and enter beneath the great portcullis.

The baronial hall was full of visitors. Clare moved slowly round, stopping before each massive portrait of a former duke, all of them in the battle-dress of the period. The walls were festooned with weapons, from the pikes and broadswords of earlier centuries to the more modern rifles and bayonets. Flags and battle emblems were draped against the huge stone walls. Flagons of leather and vessels of base and precious metals stood with goblets, plates and dishes on an enormous plank table down the centre of the hall.

A guide was conducting a party of Americans round, pointing out items of exceptional interest. Clare heard him order his party to look up and note the 'great, grand stone stairway' at the north end of the hall. Everyone, including Clare, turned their gaze towards the massive staircase, and there, halfway up, standing head and shoulders above everyone else, stood Tom.

He was looking straight at her, obviously having spotted her before she was aware of him. She waved, and he raised a hand in acknowledgement as she started wending her way through the crowd to the foot of the stairs.

She thought that he looked not unlike one of the duke's ancestors, with his noble nose and flashing blue eyes. Given a curled wig and a feathered hat, he'd have made a stunning cavalier.

He smiled his beautiful smile, took her arm and bent to kiss her as he stepped off the bottom stair. Clare returned his chaste social kiss with one of her own, though she would have liked to be folded in his arms and kissed with passion. So much for playing cool and hard to get.

He looked down at her, his eyes full of love. He put a hand under her elbow, drawing her into a dim recess at the side of the staircase. As always, his touch made her senses reel, and, as always, he knew it.

'Me too,' he said. 'Feel my heart.' He took her hand and placed it palm downwards on his chest beneath the thin cotton jacket. 'Pretend that you've got a stethoscope,' he whispered. 'Oh, darling.' He kissed her again, this time on the lips, after looking around to make sure that they were not observed. She returned it with barely restrained passion.

'Let's get out of here.' His voice was husky with emotion, his eyes the darkest blue. The grip on her elbow tightened.

'Oh,' she squeaked, 'that hurts.'

'Oh, sweeheart, I am sorry.' He loosened his hold a fraction.

'I don't mind.' She grinned up at him happily.

He stopped suddenly and some of the American group cannoned into them, sweeping them along with their party. Trying to shield her against the pressure from many bodies, he murmured, 'Aren't you supposed to be restraining me, keeping me in check?'

Clare giggled. 'That was the general idea, but I don't want to, not any more, though I want to be married. You did say that you'd marry me, in writing, and you did mean it, didn't you?'

'With all my heart. Everything that I said in my letter was true. I'm ready when you are, and I'll do it your way.'

'Then please marry me as soon as possible. I think Father would count the last few weeks as part of our courtship.'

Tom raised surprised eyebrows. 'Courtship?'

Clare explained her father's theory about a period of courtship before marriage.

'He's talking about wooing, just as I suggested,' he replied, laughing.

'Yes, I suppose he is.'

'Well, I said that I was willing and I am, dear girl. But I must say that I hope the procedure doesn't take too long, I want you so much.'

'Can you manage a month?'

'Just about,' he confirmed with a grin.

Clare said, 'I think we'd better stay with the tour of the castle—it might be safer. I don't trust myself, and certainly not you.'

'You're quite right not to, my dear; I'm going to find it hard to keep up this charade, but I will,' he ended firmly. 'It'll help, I suppose, that I'm likely to be busy at the Tropical for a while. But what are you going to do? You said on the phone that you wanted to see the castle before leaving. Leaving where, dear girl—the Cottage?'

'Yes.' She filled him in on the details. He was satisfyingly angry about the way the board had treated her.

'I'm glad that you've resigned,' he said, 'not just because it tidies things up for you and me, but because you should make a stand. It's monstrous after all you've done for the hospital that they should treat you so.'

'Would you mind if I work after we get married?'

'Not if you want to, my love, but I must admit that I'd dearly like you to myself for a bit.'

'I'll see what I can do.'

He kissed her in the shelter of an alcove halfway down the stairs to the ancient kitchens and dungeons, as the main mass of Americans surged past them.

He looked at his watch.

'When do you have to go back?' Clare asked.

'Middle of the evening. I want to monitor the medication we've put that poor guy on.'

They were at the bottom of the stairs where the corridor split into two narrow arms, one leading to the dungeons, the other to the kitchens.

'Do you really want to go on with this tour?' Tom asked.

'No; I'd like to have a cup of tea and some squashy cakes and talk about you and me.'

'Then, for heaven's sake, let's do that.'

He turned her round and took her arm. They had their feet on the first step of the steep stairs when a sudden surge of people erupted from the passage leading from the dungeons. They met the people coming down the stairs, but continued to press upwards. They looked frightened. Clare and Tom caught some of the disjointed words that were being uttered.

'It's a bomb. . .' '. . .in the dungeons. . .' '. . .a

bomb. . .' 'Lots of smoke, don't. . .' 'Fire, there's a fire!'

Very quickly the stairs and approach to the stairs was filled with men, women and children trying to escape from the dungeons below. People on the stairs were trying to turn as the flood of human beings climbed up towards them. An official voice was heard asking visitors not to panic. 'There isn't a bomb,' it said. 'Please exit in an orderly fashion.'

A spiral of smoke that soon turned into a cloud advanced down the corridor behind the fleeing visitors. The official voice, enhanced by a loud hailer, tried to reassure. 'It's only a smoke bomb, planted by a practical joker,' said the voice. 'Please cover your face with a handkerchief or scarf or something similar, and make your way to the nearest exit.'

Tom pushed Clare against the wall and stood in front of her. 'We're in more danger of being run down by the mob than the effects of the bomb,' he said, smiling down at her. 'Here——' he produced a large, snowy white handkerchief from a pocket '—put that over your beautiful little nose.' He bent and kissed the upturned tip. His calm calmed her.

'No, you have that.' She thrust the handkerchief back at him and pulled a filmy soft headsquare from her bag and tied it round her head over mouth and nose. 'This is fine for me.'

The smoke moved like a curtain towards them. 'Get down near the ground,' Tom commanded, and pulled her to her knees.

People pushed and stumbled around them. A stout little old lady with red-rimmed eyes halted, coughing and spluttering, beside them; she was holding a small white-faced boy by the hand who was clearly having difficulty breathing.

Tom stood up and swept the two of them against the

wall within the circle of his protective arms. He took off his handkerchief and bent to tie it round the boy's face. The child gasped and struggled to reject it. Clare took off her scarf and offered it to the old lady.

'I think this child's asthmatic,' said Tom, meeting Clare's eyes over the heads of the woman and boy.

The lady nodded her head. 'Me grandson, 'e's got asthma.'

'Has he got a spray or something for his breathing?' asked Tom, already searching through the terrified breathless boy's pockets. He found an inhaler and tried to help the boy use it, but he was panicking and simply pushed at it and turned his head from side to side.

During the seconds when this little drama was taking place, the tide of people pushing past them to reach the stairs continued. There seemed to be no end to the numbers of visitors desperately trying to leave the extensive dungeon area, made more difficult and hazardous by the narrow winding passages.

Tom stood up to his full height for a moment and looked along the wall. 'There's a door about six feet along,' he said to Clare. 'We'll get them there and pray that it's not locked. Anywhere out of this lot will help.'

Somehow keeping the boy and his grandmother between them, he and Clare edged along the wall against the stream of frightened people. Somebody muttered at them, 'Don't go that way, smoke'll kill you.' It was a stout elderly gentleman, and he tried to edge them back the other way, but Tom succeeded in pushing a way through and past him. The smoke was everywhere now, a great swirling mass of acrid fumes and dense greyness, a choking, irritating substance that made breathing painful.

Come with us,' he urged, 'through that door.' The man shook his head and was carried forward in the crowd.

Tom reached out and breathed a sigh of relief as the door swung open. He ushered Clare and the other two in and tried to persuade others nearby to enter, but nobody took any notice. He shut the massive oak door behind them.

The elderly lady was gasping for breath now, in almost as bad a state as her grandson, who was near collapse.

'Bronchitic?' queried Clare, trying hard to be cool and collected.

Tom nodded. 'You do what you can for her; I'll see to the boy.'

The room seemed to be a mixture of a staff-room and office. There was a door leading off marked 'Toilet', and Tom opened the door. 'Thank God,' he said, 'water.' There was even a tap marked 'Drinking Water'.

In the main room was a dresser with mugs and crockery, a kettle and tea-bags.

'We're going to be here for a while. The door will keep most of the smoke out, I think,' Tom explained to the elderly woman. 'And this lady's a nurse and I'm a doctor, so we'll do what we can for the little boy and for you.' He gave her a reassuring smile to which she responded with pathetic eagerness.

'Oh, you're a doctor! Mike'll be all right, then.' She smiled and coughed painfully, and neither Clare nor Tom had the heart to tell her that, without medication, their power to help the asthamtic child was limited.

'I'll make a cup of tea.' Clare filled the kettle and buslted round the dresser, trying to instil a feeling of normality into the situation.

Tom was holding Mike on his lap and moistening his lips with water. The child was a little less aggressive and restless now, and after a moment or two Tom persuaded him to use his ventolin inhaler. Clare thought how marvellous he was with him, infinitely patient and yet somehow managing to be firm and claim the boy's confidence. By massaging his back and chest he had persuaded him to cough up some plugs of mucous which almost immediately gave him some relief.

They could hear, even through the enormously thick door, the noise of people passing down the passage, though it seemed at last that there were fewer of them. Although it was thick, the door was ill-fitting and there was a sizeable gap at the bottom. It was Mrs Kemp who first noticed the scroll of smoke curling through the gap.

'Fetch a towel or anything you can find,' Tom instructed Clare, 'and push it hard against the crack.' He himself was unable to move without disturbing Mike, who had suddenly, through exhaustion and anxiety, fallen asleep on his lap.

She crammed tea-towels and some cleaning cloths into the gap, successfully excluding most of the smoke. An unpleasant thought went through her mind that perhaps there was a fire as well as a smoke bomb in the dungeons. Her fear must have shown in her eyes and communicated itself to Tom, for he smiled and shook his head.

'The smoke will lie around for a bit because it's in such a confined space,' he said, completely allaying her fears.

They were there for about half an hour until the fire brigade, who had been called in to deal with the smoke, arrived wearing breathing apparatus.

It was a strange half-hour. Mrs Kemp, like her grandson, exhausted by the events of the afternoon and comforted by a cup of tea and Clare's reassuring grip on her hand, also fell asleep. Tom and Clare conducted a whispered conversation about the possible reasons for the throwing of the smoke bomb, the condition of their two charges and whether either would suffer any ill-effects from the experience. The words were ordinary enough, but in a way they were having a conversation about their love for each other.

There was still smoke hanging about in clouds near the ceiling when the fire brigade rescued them. They'd brought extra breathing apparatus with them, which they used for Mike and Mrs Kemp.

It was extraordinary coming out into the hot bright sunshine after the chill and dimness of the dungeons.

Mrs Kemp was loudly vocal in her praise of their help.

''E's a doctor and the young lady's a nurse,' she told the firemen as they carried her from the basement, and added dramatically, 'We'd 'ave died if it 'adn't been for them, Mike and me.'

There were a lot of people milling about at the top of the stairs in the great hall, newspaper men among them. They recognised a couple of reporters from local papers.

Remembering their experiences after the river rescue, they asked a castle worker to guide them out through one of the numerous back exits to avoid the waiting Press and other media.

They were directed down a narrow passasge which ended at a heavy oak door studded with nails. It opened on to a small paved courtyard with another door in the cobbled wall. This in turn opened on to the hill at the back of the castle.

The hill rose almost vertically behind the wall. There were a few steep steps cut roughly into the turf at the start of a track that zig-zagged up the hill. Tom went first, occasionally reaching back to give Clare a pull. They arrived at the top, exhilarated but breathless. It was wonderful to breathe the fresh air after their enforced captivity.

'Well, well,' said Tom, looking pleased. 'I couldn't have planned it better if I'd tried.'

'Planned what?'

'Wait and see, my darling; we must go just a little further to that copse of trees.'

In the middle of the cluster of trees stood the ruins of what might have been a small chapel.

'It's called The Lover's Knot, or My Lady's Bower,' Tom explained. Clare looked disbelieving. 'Honestly, love; look, it's here in the castle booklet. But I had no idea that this is where we would end up.'

He took a paperback brochure from his pocket and flicked it open at the appropriate page. Sure enough there was a picture of the ruins and a caption beneath stating that they were so called.

'Apparently,' he said, 'one of the early dukes built this little chapel-like building for his lady wife. Before he went off to the Crusades or some other battle they would renew their wedding vows and have a mass said for his safe return. His wife would watch for his homecoming from a window embrasure in the turret. She could see the estuary and watch him sail back up the river and wait for him to join her here.'

'How romantic,' sighed Clare, her usual practical self deserting her. 'He must have loved her very much.'

'Almost as much as I love you.' Tom turned her to face him and, before she could protest, lifted her up and sat her on the ruined wall of the turret.

He wasn't on his knees before her, but for the first time since their meeting in her office aeons ago she could look down on him. His upturned face looked lean and brown, and the expression in his amazing blue eyes yearning, loving. He took a small box from his jacket pocket and opened it.

He held it up that she might see it easily. On a satin cushion lay an old ring. A glowing rose-pink gem surrounded by seed pearls that reflected the light and colour of the mother stone on a bed of antique whirling silver threads.

'Oh, it's beautiful. . . I've never seen anything like it before.'

'Nor ever will again, dear girl. My grandfather had it made for my grandmother when he was courting her. There, your father's word. It was meant to be a keepsake, but she insisted on wearing it as an engagement ring. Will you accept it as an engagement ring, Clare?'

She couldn't speak for a moment, and her eyes filled with tears so that she saw his dear face through a misty veil.

At last she whispered, 'Yes, please.'

Tom reached up and took her left hand and placed the circlet on her ring finger. He kissed it and kissed her palm, and then lifted up his arms and plucked her from her perch. She put her arms around his neck and pulled his head down until their lips touched and they kissed each other hungrily.

They drew apart at last, and Tom said with a mixture of regret and humour, 'I'll have to go, love of my life; duty calls.'

'To your other love,' said Clare.

'Jealous?'

'Not of your patients, but of the time you must give them.'

'Inevitable, I'm afraid.'

'I can live with it,' she said cheerfully.

'Love you,' he said. He touched her cheek with his fingers.

'And I you,' said Clare as, hand in hand, they walked down the hill.

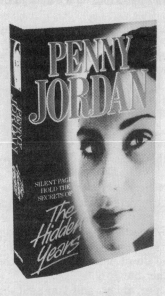

—MEDICAL  ROMANCE—

The books for your enjoyment this month are:

AND DARE TO DREAM Elisabeth Scott
DRAGON LADY Stella Whitelaw
TROPICAL PARADISE Margaret Barker
COTTAGE HOSPITAL Margaret O'Neill

♥   ♥   ♥   ♥   ♥

Treats in store!

Watch next month for the following absorbing stories:

CROCK OF GOLD Angela Devine
SEIZE THE DAY Sharon Wirdnam
LEARNING TO CARE Clare Mackay
FROM SHADOW TO SUNLIGHT Jenny Ashe